A terrible fall could spell disaster…

Christina's heart jumped to her throat as she felt herself being flipped out of the saddle. She had lost her right stirrup during Charisma's sideways leap. As the filly made a valiant effort to position herself in the air, Christina knew there was no way she would keep her seat when the filly landed. Wanting to fall clear of the filly, she let go of the reins. Charisma's front legs hit the track, catapulting Christina over her left side. Christina's left foot remained in the stirrup. Panicked, Christina struggled to free her left leg, but she couldn't. Her boot was caught in the iron.

Christina landed hard on the thick dirt of the Belmont track. Her left ankle twisted painfully in the stirrup, and white spots blurred her vision. As the spots selectively cleared, Christina had a perfect view of the clear, bright blue sky and cirrus clouds that looked like horse tails. Then Charisma went down, and everything faded to black.

Collect all the books in the Thoroughbred series

Collect all the books in the Ashleigh series

*coming soon

THOROUGHBRED

Breaking the Fall

CREATED BY

JOANNA CAMPBELL

WRITTEN BY

JENNIFER CHU

HarperEntertainment
An Imprint of HarperCollinsPublishers

HarperEntertainment
An Imprint of HarperCollins*Publishers*
10 East 53rd Street, New York, NY 10022-5299

Produced by 17th Street Productions,
an Alloy Online, Inc., company

ISBN 0-06-073812-X

First printing: September 2004

Printed in the United States of America

Visit HarperEntertainment on the World Wide Web at
www.harpercollins.com

❖ 10 9 8 7 6 5 4 3 2 1

To John, for supporting me in everything I do

BREAKING THE FALL

"LADIES AND GENTLEMEN, THIS IS THE CAPTAIN SPEAKING."
The crackling voice over the airplane intercom made Christina Reese look up from her reading. "I apologize again for the delay. Because of the current weather conditions, we are still waiting for air traffic control to clear us for landing. We should have you on the ground in roughly forty-five minutes."

Christina capped her highlighter with a sigh and closed her biology textbook. How could she possibly concentrate on the intricacies of DNA replication when she was this close to Belmont Park and a reunion with her horse, Wonder's Star?

Everyone else at Whitebrook Farm, the Thoroughbred breeding and training facility Christina's parents owned, had left for Belmont three days before, but Christina had stayed behind to take a chemistry test. Although she had decided not to go to college full-time this year because she wanted to focus on her jockeying career, Christina had registered for a couple of introductory science classes at the local community college. Since she was still considering veterinary school, she knew she needed a solid science background.

Christina looked out the airplane window. Her mind wandered to the events of the past few months as her eyes skimmed over the foggy haze of lights beneath the clouds.

Some of the best and worst moments in Christina's racing career had occurred over the summer. It had begun on a high note: Star's victory in the Belmont Stakes, the last leg of the Triple Crown. But less than two weeks later, a horrible accident had occurred. One of Christina's favorite horses, Calm Before the Storm, had broken down at the end of the Riva Ridge Breeders' Cup and had later been euthanized at an equine surgery clinic.

Christina had felt so helpless afterward. She'd thought about quitting racing and becoming a vet so that she could work with horses in pain, like Callie. After talking with the veterinarian who had operated on Callie, though, Christina realized that she wasn't ready to make any decisions about her future quite yet. Besides, how could she stop racing before Star's career was over?

Christina smiled as she thought about Star. She'd loved the handsome chestnut colt from the moment he was born.

Star was the last foal out of Ashleigh's Wonder. Christina's mother, Ashleigh Griffen, had turned Wonder from a sickly foal to a champion racer and had watched many of the mare's offspring become champions in their own right. Wonder had died shortly after Star's birth, and from that point on, Christina wanted to help Star be the best race-horse he could be in Wonder's honor. At first, looking at Star had been too painful for Ashleigh, since the colt reminded her so much of Wonder, but in the past two years she'd come to love Star almost as much as Christina did, and had even helped Christina design the training plan that had made Star a competitive three-year-old racer.

Ashleigh's training plan had put Star on track to win the Travers Stakes in August, but Christina had been forced to scratch Star from that race because of an overeager fan who had followed the colt to Saratoga. For Star's safety, Christina had even boarded him at Whitebrook's rival farm, Townsend Acres, for a few weeks. Moving Star to Townsend Acres had come at a price, though—the owner, Brad Townsend, had threatened to take control of Christina's cousin's horse, Perfect Image, if Christina moved Star off the farm. Fortunately, Christina had managed to negotiate both Image's and Star's freedom in exchange for Star's winnings from the Belmont Stakes.

Since Christina had moved Star back to Whitebrook a month before, things had been pretty calm. Christina had managed to strike a balance between doing her school-work, training Star for his fall races, and helping Samantha

3

Nelson, a family friend, prepare for the birth of twins. But now that the Belmont fall meet had begun, things were going to get a lot more hectic. Christina didn't mind, though; she was looking forward to racing horses for Whitebrook as well as for other training farms.

The next day Christina would be riding in two races. The first was the maiden race for Enigmatic, a colt sired by Charismatic, who had almost won the Triple Crown in 1999. Enigmatic was owned by Patrick and Amanda Johnston of Dreamflight Racing Farm. Christina had ridden several races for Dreamflight that summer and had a good relationship with the Johnstons, even though they had also been Callie's owners and trainers. Christina's second race would be on her favorite two-year-old at Whitebrook, a big filly named Charisma. Charisma had won almost every race she'd been entered in so far, and the next day the filly would be running in her first grade I race, the Matron Stakes.

As excited as Christina was about these upcoming races, though, the race she was most looking forward to was the Jockey Club Gold Cup. The Gold Cup would be Star's final race before the Breeders' Cup Classic. Christina was imagining what might happen if he did well there when her reverie was interrupted by the voice of a flight attendant on the loudspeaker.

"Ladies and gentlemen, the captain has informed me that we have been cleared for landing. In preparation, please make sure that your carry-on items are stowed, your seat belts are fastened, and your seats are in the upright position.

Also we ask that you turn off any electronic devices at this time. We hope to have you on the ground shortly."

Christina turned away from the window and stuffed her textbook in her backpack. She squirmed in her seat, suddenly unable to sit still. She couldn't wait to get off the plane and to her beloved horse!

"And so everything is going well until my horse decides that he should try to attack the wire rather than cross under it," Melanie said. She used some silverware to reenact the scene from her morning workout. The fork bounced up and down, trying to reach the stationary knife that served as the finish line.

Christina laughed, nearly choking on a bite of salad. She had originally planned to join Patrick and Amanda Johnston for dinner, but because of her flight delay she hadn't been able to make it. Instead she and Melanie were grabbing a late meal at a local diner, which was actually a lot more fun.

"How did you convince Jinx to calm down?" Christina asked.

"Calm down? Jinx?" Melanie gestured wildly with the fork. "He had to convince himself that this wasn't a battle he could win. I'm telling you, if I didn't love that silly horse so much . . ."

Christina gave a sympathetic chuckle, even though she couldn't entirely relate. While Star's early training had not been without its difficulties, she certainly couldn't match her cousin's experiences. The first horse Melanie had trained was Perfect Image, a headstrong black filly who could not tolerate stalls, horse trailers, most other horses, or much of anything at all. But Melanie had found ways to accommodate the filly's quirks and had turned her into a Kentucky Derby winner. Unfortunately, Image's racing career had ended with that race, when the filly broke down at the wire and almost died.

Now Melanie had a new horse, a chestnut fireball named Hi Jinx. Jinx had shown his ability to run, but he also had a mean streak, biting grooms and destroying stalls. Melanie was getting through to him slowly—she had guided him to victory in the Kentucky Cup the previous month. Yet despite his recent improvements, Jinx still had his wild moments. Only a week earlier he had kicked through a rail in the paddock fence at Whitebrook.

Melanie picked up her sandwich and sank back in her chair, blowing a lock of her blond hair out of her face in frustration.

"Everything okay?" Christina wondered.

Melanie shrugged. "Well, at least the clocker stopped the time before Jinx's explosion, so he put in some good numbers. The other Futurity Stakes entrants won't be able to write us off." But Melanie still looked troubled.

"You're going to do great next week," Christina reassured her. "Jinx was unstoppable in the Kentucky Cup."

"Jinx was awesome in that race," Melanie replied as she

picked at her baked potato. "But I don't know how well he's going to handle the next three Jazz wants to enter him in."

"The next three?" Christina knew that Jazz Taylor, who was Melanie's boyfriend and owned both Image and Jinx, was under financial pressure. Jazz was the lead singer in the band Pegasus. The band had been very popular during the previous year, but their latest album wasn't selling very well. Between the costs of the band's recent European tour and the veterinary bills associated with Image's recovery, Jazz was counting on his investment in Jinx to pay off.

"Jazz is insisting that Jinx earn his keep, and he thinks Jinx needs to win three more races as a two-year-old to do that."

Christina took another bite of salad as she tried to think of a suitable reply. A few months before, she never would have imagined that Jazz would act this way. He had been completely devoted to Melanie as well as to Image. In fact, at a June concert in Lexington, he had performed a song he had written about the two of them. But Christina knew that Jazz's financial stresses and his recent interest in selling Image to Brad had strained the relationship between him and Melanie. "Have you tried telling Jazz that Jinx would do better in the long run if he had more time to mature?"

"He won't listen," Melanie said. "He just keeps telling me he doesn't need money later, he needs money *now*. He's already taking out loans so that his band can go back into the recording studio. And when I bring up the idea of ending Jinx's two-year-old season early, he starts to talk about selling him." Melanie sighed. "I hope we'll work something out soon. But I don't want to talk about this. Let's talk about you. How did that chemistry test go?"

"All right, I think," Christina answered, deciding to let Melanie off the hook. "Though I should have done more practice problems. How has Star been doing?"

"Fine. We did a short work on the track this morning. I can tell he misses you. He's turning into more of a one-person horse. I mean, I can't imagine him doing nearly as well for me in a race as he does for you."

"You never know. You've won on him before," Christina pointed out. Melanie had ridden Star in a big race during his two-year-old season because Christina had been committed to another mount.

"That was a long time ago," Melanie said. "You two have been through so much together since then. I couldn't imagine you ever letting someone race him again."

"Yeah, I definitely plan to ride Star for the rest of his races," Christina said. "But I'll always need help exercising him, so it's great that I can count on people like you." Christina finished the last of her sandwich. "Okay, enough talking about Star. Let's go see him!"

At the sound of Star's familiar whinny, Christina broke into a jog down the long barn aisle. Star held his sculpted head over his stall door, and Christina put her arms around his neck.

"Hey, Star! I missed you, boy."

Star nudged Christina and lipped at her red-brown hair.

"Melanie said that you missed me, too. Did you?" Christina asked. She dug into her pocket for some carrot sticks she had saved from dinner.

Star chomped on the carrots eagerly and then nosed Christina's pockets, looking for more. Laughing, Christina let herself into Star's stall. Once inside, she ran a hand down Star's back and flank. "You know, boy, every time I look at you, I wonder how I could even think about leaving racing to be a vet."

Star nickered, leaning into Christina's caresses. Christina would have been content to spoil Star with attention and food all night, but a few minutes later she heard footsteps in the aisle. As the footsteps came closer, she recognized the voices of her mother and Cindy McLean, the head trainer at Tall Oaks, a neighboring racing farm. The low tones told her they were having a serious discussion.

Ashleigh stuck her head over the stall door. "I thought I'd find you here, Chris," she said. "Do I get a hug, or are those reserved for your favorite horse?"

"Of course you get a hug." Christina fed Star one last carrot before leaving his stall. "What were you two just gossiping about?" she asked teasingly.

Ashleigh and Cindy exchanged glances. Then Ashleigh answered, "Samantha's twins," just as Cindy said, "Ben's trip to Dubai."

Before Christina could ask what was really going on, Cindy's cell phone rang. Cindy checked the number and quickly excused herself, saying she had to take the call.

"Is Ben's trip going well?" Christina asked her mother after Cindy had left. Ben al-Rihani was the owner of Tall Oaks. He and Cindy had been dating for the past six months, but Christina still wasn't sure how serious the relationship was.

There was a complicated history between Cindy and Ben. Cindy had once worked in Dubai for Ben's father, an Arabian sheik, but had left when the sheik made it clear that he was not interested in having women ride his horses. Ben was far more progressive than his father, but Christina knew that Cindy was still trying to balance working for him and dating him.

For the past two weeks Cindy had been running Tall Oaks while Ben was in Dubai looking at horses that he might want to import. His return had been delayed twice already, but he was scheduled to be back by the end of the week.

"Yeah, everything's fine. He's still planning to come back on Saturday," Ashleigh replied quickly. She reached over the stall door to pat Star. "Anyway, I've been watching the workouts of some of the other Gold Cup entrants, and it looks like Star is going to have some stiff competition, especially from the older horses."

Star had run only against three-year-olds so far this season, so Christina had not been following the older horses as closely. "I don't think the Johnstons are entering Matter of Time," she said, referring to the four-year-old who had won the previous year's Breeders' Cup Classic. "Who will be running?"

"Well, there's a West Coast horse named Magic Trick. He did well at Santa Anita in the spring, and he blew away the field in the Whitney. And there's Storm Rider, of course."

Christina nodded gravely. Storm Rider—a huge New York–bred colt—had narrowly beaten her and Matter of Time in the Suburban Handicap at the beginning of the summer. "Anyone else I should be watching?"

Ashleigh shook her head. "There's a late-blooming three-year-old named Stronghold who did well at Arlington, but I think his owners are skipping the Gold Cup and just waiting until the Classic."

Christina leaned against the stall door glumly. "If I hadn't panicked and scratched Star before the Travers, we might have been able to give him a break before the Classic."

"You did what you thought was best," Ashleigh assured her. "And Star was pretty upset."

"But we had him in perfect shape before the Travers," Christina said. Although she had initially argued against her mother's light summer training plan, the slower works and trail rides had helped Star regain his fitness after the Triple Crown.

"And he's in great shape now. Your breeze times last week were among the best they've ever been." Ashleigh's words were punctuated by several of Star's nickers. "You see, he agrees with me. Quit worrying so much."

Christina smiled, trying to push aside her concerns. Perhaps her mother was right, but she would have to wait until the Gold Cup to know for sure.

2

BEEP. BEEP. BEEP.

The soft but insistent buzzing of the alarm clock woke Christina from a deep sleep. Groaning, she rolled over and hit the snooze button. She was exhausted, but after a moment she forced herself to get up.

Thirty minutes later Christina was glad she hadn't let herself sleep in. She hadn't done the best job packing, and she had to scour her luggage to find the items that she needed for a day at the track.

"Mel, have you seen my hair ties?" Christina asked frantically as she stood in front of the mirror, trying to brush her hair. Looking in the mirror, she noticed that there were faint circles under her hazel eyes. *I'll have to get some more sleep before Parker gets here*, she thought.

Christina's boyfriend, Parker Townsend, had spent the past three months in England, training with the famous Jack Dalton in preparation for the Burghley horse trials. Burghley was one of the most prestigious three-day events in the world, and Parker and his horse, Foxglove, had placed fourth. Now that the event was over, Parker was returning to the United States. When Christina had talked to him two days earlier, he had said he would stop by Belmont on his way to New Jersey, where he would be talking with some of the heads of the United States Equestrian Team. Since Parker had received a special award for being the top rider under age twenty-five at Burghley, he was getting a lot more attention from key people in the eventing world.

"Calm down, Chris. There are some hair ties in your toiletries bag," Melanie replied. Melanie kept her blond hair short, so she never had to bother with things like that. "Why are you so keyed up this morning?"

"I don't know. I think I'm just excited to be back at the track." As she pulled her hair back into a low ponytail, Christina went through the plans for her day in her head. She would work Star first. Then she was scheduled to breeze two horses for Dreamflight and another three for Tall Oaks. She also wanted to spend some time walking around the barns before the day's races began, since she needed to talk with other trainers about getting mounts.

During the summer Christina had tried to get her name out as a jockey. Many trainers still seemed reluctant to hire her because of her youth, but her Belmont win had definitely opened some doors. Christina hoped that she would be able to open more doors during this meet, because she could use the money. When Star had won the Belmont, Christina had thought she would never need to worry about money again. But now those winnings were in Brad's hands.

"You ready to go, Chris?" Melanie asked.

Christina brushed some of the loose hair out of her face. "Yeah, I'm ready."

"Everything all right?"

Christina nodded. She had made Brad promise not to tell Melanie about the deal they had made for Image's freedom, since she didn't want her cousin to feel guilty about what had happened. "Come on. Let's get out there and ride."

The Belmont track stretched out in a long ribbon before Christina. Flash thunderstorms earlier in the week had colored the dirt a few shades darker, and there were still heavy patches where the horses' hooves made sucking sounds as they walked. For Christina, none of this took away from the beauty. She had always loved the Belmont oval. At a mile and a half, it was longer than most tracks around the country, but she liked the wide, sweeping turns. Four months earlier she had used these turns to her advantage, gaining ground and giving Star a chance to win the Belmont Stakes.

As she and Star completed the circuit at a canter, Christina couldn't help smiling as she remembered that moment. She crouched over Star's withers and clucked. "Let's gallop, boy!" she called, giving the colt rein.

Star easily changed gears, moving from his liquid-smooth canter to a ground-eating gallop. For the first time since she had arrived at Belmont, Christina relaxed. This was where she belonged.

The mile markers blurred as Christina and Star flew past. Ashleigh's instructions had called for a half-mile gallop followed by a half-mile breeze, and Christina looked up the track eagerly, wanting to release Star's full potential.

As they approached the half-mile marker Christina slid her hands slightly up Star's neck and clucked again. This was all the encouragement Star needed. He shot forward, determined to defeat even the wind.

Christina lost herself in the rapid rhythm of Star's strides, so even and sure despite the poor track conditions. Since Callie's accident, she knew she would never be able to take this feeling for granted again.

"Attaboy, Star!" Christina encouraged as they rounded the far turn. Star acted as if he was charging toward the finish line in an actual race. His neck was flat and extended, and his long copper legs were covering more ground with each stride. He even changed leads down the homestretch, clicking into high gear just as he streaked past the finish point.

Christina couldn't stop smiling as she rode back to her

mother. She knew this had been one of their best breezes this month. She leaned down to pat Star. "I really missed that, boy."

"That was amazing, Chris," Ashleigh praised, looking at a stopwatch. "If you and Star keep getting times like this, you're going to be unstoppable."

Christina shrugged. "Star did the work. All I had to do was stay on." She took off her riding gloves and patted her colt again, enjoying the feeling of his short coat against her fingers. "Now I'd better go find the Johnstons and Cindy so that I can ride their horses. I'll meet you back at the barn to go over our strategy for Charisma's race." Before she dismounted, Christina gave Star one last pat. "Thanks for a great work, boy," she said softly. "I can't wait for our next two races."

Although there was always a lot going on at the track, the intensity ramped up when the races began. Christina noticed the commotion as she walked out of the relative quiet of the jockeys' lounge to the walking ring. Enigmatic's maiden race was the first race on the day's card, and bettors were trying to get one last look before putting their money on these unproven horses.

Luckily, Patrick Johnston had managed to clear a space near the center of the ring for Enigmatic. One of Dreamflight's grooms, Jessica, stood at the colt's head, walking him in a tight circle. Christina made her way to them purposefully, tuning out the background conversation.

"He looks good," Christina said, trying to keep the nervous catch out of her voice. She wondered if she would ever stop being anxious before a race. Part of her hoped that she would one day control the butterflies, but another part wasn't sure. After all, if she stopped getting nervous, would that mean the races were less important?

"Yeah, he's taking all of this pretty well," Patrick replied. "Enigmatic's never minded people. He just doesn't like crowds of horses."

"Should I be worried about that?" Christina asked.

"I'm not sure you'll be able to keep him out of traffic. Just try to keep his mind on running and do the best you can," Patrick instructed. He gave Christina a leg up into the saddle. "I'm not expecting a win. I just want him to get some experience."

Christina slid her right foot into the stirrup, lifting herself above the saddle. While most young horses tended to get skittish when a rider put weight on their backs, Enigmatic only took a couple of sideways steps. "I'll do my best," she promised.

Patrick patted Enigmatic's neck. "Have a good ride."

"And they're off!" The announcer's voice rang in Christina's ears as Enigmatic lunged from the gate. Enigmatic broke off balance, pushing harder with his left hind leg than his right, but Christina quickly angled him toward the rail. As Enigmatic settled into a ground-eating gallop along the rail, Christina could feel the earlier bubble of nervousness in her stomach dissolve into excitement. She saw a gap right along the rail and pointed Enigmatic toward it. The colt responded smoothly, tugging on the reins as he saw the running room before him.

"Easy, boy," Christina said, running a hand along the colt's neck. "We'll get our chance." As Christina scanned the track for gaps that would indicate the lead horses were slowing, she heard snatches of the announcer's comments.

"At the quarter mile, it's Carry Me Home in the lead, with Question Everything gaining ground. Tight Junction is half a length back in third, followed by Reflective and Freefall. Further back, Enigmatic leads the closers. . . ."

Christina let Enigmatic out a notch. Because the race was only six furlongs, she couldn't afford to wait too long to make her move. Enigmatic lengthened his stride, quickly passing Freefall. He was about to pass Reflective when a tiring Tight Junction drifted toward the rail, blocking the opening.

Enigmatic tossed his head, giving a small buck. Christina got the colt's attention with a few quick tugs of the rein. "You're okay, boy," she soothed, trying to stay balanced despite the colt's movements.

The colt didn't listen. He threw his head up again, protesting Christina's pull. "It's all right," Christina repeated.

"I'm trying to get us out of here, but I need you to calm down." Christina felt a twinge of panic as she glanced around the track. The lead horses were dropping back, and the closers were picking up the pace. If she didn't get Enigmatic under control soon, they would be caught in an even bigger pack, and there was no telling how the colt would react.

Christina looked to either side. Despite Enigmatic's erratic gait, he had managed to pass Reflective. Christina applied pressure with her inside leg, trying to get the colt to move away from the cue. For a moment it felt as though Enigmatic would fight her and throw himself in the opposite direction. The horse's muscles tightened like springs, quivering with tension.

Christina repeated her cues, trying to get Enigmatic to the outside. They wouldn't be able to make up the ground to win if they took that path, but at least she would be able to end Enigmatic's first race on a positive note.

Enigmatic tossed his head one last time and then made a half-shying motion toward the outside. This was all Christina needed to reassert her presence. She used Enigmatic's momentum to get the colt around Question Everything, who was drifting wide, and then the track in front of them was clear.

Seeing all the open space ahead, Enigmatic needed no more than a quick flick of the crop to start running. He dashed forward, accelerating with every stride. As they rounded the far turn, Christina saw a horse fly by to the inside, but she did not pull Enigmatic toward the rail. Instead she gave the colt his head, letting him run along the outside path.

As they pounded down the homestretch Christina knew that the wide turn had cost them too much valuable ground. Yet she kept encouraging Enigmatic. She really wanted to show the colt how wonderful it was to race. She was so intent on helping Enigmatic run that she was barely aware of crossing under the wire. Looking ahead, she saw two other jockeys slowing their horses.

"Third place, boy. That's not too bad for your first time," Christina said, patting the colt's neck. She could feel the untapped reserves of the colt beneath her. "I bet you're going to be amazing on the track next year, just like your father was." Enigmatic's sire, Charismatic, had surprised the racing world by winning the first two races of the Triple Crown in 1999. However, Charismatic had broken down in the Belmont Stakes and had never raced again. Callie's death and Image's accident had made Christina reflect on famous horses that had ended their careers by breaking down on the track. Looking at Enigmatic, Christina felt that Charismatic's story would ultimately be one of the more uplifting ones.

Two hours later Christina had changed from the green-and-white diamond-patterned silks of Dreamflight to the more familiar blue-and-white silks of Whitebrook and was waiting for the start of the Matron Stakes. As Christina circled Charisma behind the starting gates, she went over the instructions her mother had given her in the walking ring.

There were two speed horses in the race, Running Wild and Halo Delight. Ashleigh had warned her not to get into a duel with them. She wanted Christina to wait for the half-mile marker before making her move.

Beneath Christina, Charisma was prancing in place. Unlike Enigmatic, she tended to get keyed up before a race. "Save it for the race, girl," Christina said, stroking the filly. "I know you're going to be the best horse out there."

Charisma bobbed her head and nickered.

"That's right. You're going to make them eat your dust." Christina smiled. While the past few weeks at Whitebrook had been fun, it felt so good to be back at the track. And this day was just the beginning. She had so many exciting races in front of her!

A track attendant took Charisma's reins, leading the filly toward the gate. Charisma took a few shuddering strides away from the clanging metal before allowing Christina to guide her in. The attendant slammed the doors behind them.

Christina quickly readied herself for the start, grabbing a large chunk of Charisma's mane between her gloved fingers. She crouched over the filly's neck, anticipating a fast, hard break.

Taking a deep, calming breath, Christina started to exhale just as the bell rang and the gates slammed open with a metallic thud. Charisma broke cleanly, taking Christina to the front of the pack. Remembering Ashleigh's advice, Christina checked the filly. She wanted Charisma to relax in the middle of the pack.

Charisma obeyed her rider after a brief protest, shortening her stride. Christina glanced under her shoulder and saw Halo Delight coming up on their outside, headed to join Running Wild in the lead. Seeing the other filly breeze past her, Charisma again began fighting Christina. The filly braced against Christina's restraint, matching Halo Delight stride for stride.

"Slow down, girl. We'll catch her later." Christina angled Charisma toward the rail. The filly took an uneven step as she moved toward the sloppier part of the track. Christina was surprised at how the track conditions had deteriorated since the first race of the day.

Halo Delight's jockey moved his mount toward the rail as well. Christina wanted to slow Charisma so that the other filly could pass, but Charisma, suddenly spooked by her inability to get traction on the slippery ground, was not listening.

Charisma took another lurching stride just as Halo Delight lost her footing. Out of the corner of her eye, Christina saw the horrific blur of Halo Delight going down. One of the horse's thrashing hooves clipped Charisma's hind legs, and Charisma leaped sideways.

Christina's heart jumped to her throat as she felt herself being flipped out of the saddle. She had lost her right stirrup during Charisma's sideways leap. As the filly made a valiant effort to position herself in the air, Christina knew there was no way she would keep her seat when the filly landed. Wanting to fall clear of the filly, she let go of the reins. Charisma's front legs hit the track, catapulting Christina over her left side. Christina's left foot remained in the stirrup. Panicked, Christina struggled to free her left leg, but she couldn't. Her boot was caught in the iron.

Christina landed hard on the thick dirt of the Belmont track. Her left ankle twisted painfully in the stirrup, and white spots blurred her vision. As the spots selectively cleared, Christina had a perfect view of the clear, bright blue sky and cirrus clouds that looked like horse tails. Then Charisma went down, and everything faded to black.

3

"Eighteen-year-old female . . . racetrack accident. Displaced fractures . . . left medial and lateral malleolus . . . high fibula fracture . . . unconscious on scene . . . head and neck cleared . . . morphine in the field . . ."

Christina felt as though she were drowning. There were voices just above the water, but the waves of blackness kept washing over her.

"Your daughter's ankle . . . ligaments . . . surgery . . ."

The voices were unfamiliar, yet Christina struggled to find her way back to them. She thought she could make it to the surface, but she kept being pushed down.

"Please take good care of her."

A familiar voice this time. Her mother's voice. "Mom?"

Christina wasn't sure if anyone heard. She tried to force the word out. "Mom?"

"Christina, honey, I'm here." Ashleigh squeezed her hand.

Christina tried to open her sticky eyelids. Her mother's face was a vague, grayish blur outlined against a spinning background. Frightened, she tugged at Ashleigh's hand.

"It's going to be okay, honey," Ashleigh soothed. "You're going to be okay."

"We should get her up to surgery," a male voice said firmly.

"Just give me a second to explain. Chris, your ankle is badly damaged. They're taking you to the operating room so that you'll be able to get better faster. Do you understand?"

Christina could feel the blackness trying to take her again. It crept at the edges of her vision. She squeezed her mother's hand harder, trying to fight it off. "What happened . . ." Her voice trailed off. She was losing this fight. "Charisma?"

The blackness swallowed her before she could hear her mother's reply.

When Christina surfaced the next time, there were three familiar voices.

"Christina." The first voice echoed through the blackness, breaking it up. "Christina, honey, can you hear me?"

Someone put a hand over hers. Christina moved her fingers in response. She wanted the hand to pull her out.

The murmur of voices grew louder.

"Chris, can you wake up a little?" Melanie's voice was higher than usual.

"Mel?" Christina croaked.

"Christina, thank goodness . . ." Christina felt her mother squeeze her left hand. Had her mother done that earlier, or had it been her imagination?

"What happened?" Christina opened her eyes slowly, wincing at the blinding white light.

"You're in the hospital, Chris," Ashleigh replied gently. She leaned over so that Christina could see her. "You and Charisma went down in the Matron Stakes."

The scene replayed itself before Christina's clouded eyes. Halo Delight hitting Charisma . . . the frantic leap . . . falling . . .

Christina blinked hard several times, an act that both stopped the nightmare and significantly cleared her vision. "Charisma?" Christina felt a lump growing in the back of her throat. *Please let her be all right. Please don't tell me she died.*

Christina's father, Mike Reese, walked closer to the bed so that he was in Christina's visual field. "Charisma's perfectly fine," her father reassured her. "She was pretty shaken up, and there were some deep cuts and bruises, but she's going to be all right."

Christina stared at her father, trying to comprehend the words. Was Charisma really okay after that awful accident?

27

"It's the truth, Chris," Melanie chimed in. "Charisma's going to be fine."

Christina let out a sigh of relief. "So we were both lucky, then."

No one spoke.

Christina tried to raise her head to see what had happened, but movement caused sharp bolts of pain to shoot through her. "What aren't you telling me?" she asked, her voice rising in fear despite her weakness.

Ashleigh began smoothing Christina's hair, just the way she had done when Christina had been much younger and needed comfort. "Your left foot got caught in the stirrup when you fell," Ashleigh began. Christina could hear the hesitation in her mother's voice. "Your ankle took most of the stress of Charisma's fall." Ashleigh tightened her grip on Christina's hand.

"What your mother's trying to say was that you had surgery last night," Mike said gently. "Because your ankle was twisted under Charisma, one of the ankle bones was fractured in four places. You also broke a bone higher in your leg and tore two ligaments."

Christina's memories of her last conversation with her mother came rushing back. They had been taking her to the operating room. "How long until I can ride?" she asked raggedly.

"We don't know, Chris," Ashleigh replied softly.

"What do you mean?" Christina cried. Why wasn't anyone giving her a direct answer?

"It's going to be a while," Ashleigh admitted.

"But what about Star? What about the Classic?" Christina blinked to clear the tears that were stinging her eyes.

"The doctors don't think you're going to be riding again this year," Mike said. "Right now your ankle's in a long cast that covers nearly your whole leg. In about a month they're going to replace that with a shorter cast, which will stay on for another month. Then once everything heals, you'll need an operation to remove some of the pins that are holding your bones in place. After that, you'll be able to start rehabilitation."

Christina shook her head in denial. "But I'll be able to ride Star next year, right?"

"It depends," Ashleigh answered. "If everything goes perfectly, the doctors say you could be back on the track in as little as six months. But they've also told me that there are usually some complications, and seven or eight months could be a more realistic estimate."

For a moment Christina thought she was blacking out again. "This can't be happening! What about Star? What about all the races we had planned?"

"Let's try not to think about that right now," Mike said. "Right now the most important thing is that you're okay. For a few seconds yesterday we didn't know what to expect."

"How can I not think about it?" Christina demanded, her voice harsh with suppressed sobs. "Star's been the only thing I've thought about for the past three years! We've worked so hard. I can't let him down."

"You're not letting him down," Melanie said. "And we all know that you're going to do everything you can so that you can ride him again."

"But what if that's not enough?" Tears began trickling down Christina's cheeks. She didn't try to hide them. "What if I can't race Star again? What if I can't ride any horse?" That thought only added to Christina's bubbling hysteria. "Everything in my life is better when I'm working with Star. What if I can't do that?" Christina could barely talk through her crying. She couldn't stop the sobs from spilling out along with her words, even though they racked her sore muscles with pain. "What if everything I've worked for is over?"

Her parents and cousin moved to comfort her, but Christina shook them off, flailing her arms weakly to get them to leave her alone. Her sobs were violent now. "I've failed Star so many times already. And now I've done it again. We can't be finished now—not when we just got started!"

Starlight was filtering in through the window when Christina awakened many hours later. As her red, swollen eyes tried to focus, Christina realized that she was alone.

Slowly Christina's clouded mind wandered back to what had happened earlier. She was severely injured. It would be months before she could ride Star again. A persistent throbbing in her ankle punctuated those horrible facts.

Outside the room, Christina could hear her parents and Melanie talking.

"Do you think we should go in and check on her?" Ashleigh asked worriedly.

"We'd better just let her rest for a while," Mike replied. "The doctor said that she needs sleep. She's got a lot of physical and emotional healing to do."

"It's going to be hard on her," Melanie said. Melanie's voice sounded strange—almost as though she had been crying, too. "She loves Star so much. If I were in her place, I would be just as upset as she was."

"It was difficult to see her like that," Mike said. "But I think you told her the right thing, Mel."

"The right thing about what?" Melanie asked.

"The Christina we all know is going to put everything she has into rehab. She'll probably be on Star before any of us expects her to."

Christina felt tears well up in her eyes at that comment. After the way she had treated everyone, they still rallied behind her. She promised herself that she would apologize the next morning.

Lifting her head slightly, Christina noticed several items on her nightstand. The first was a huge arrangement of red and white roses. Beneath the flowers, there were two cards with her name on them.

Clumsily Christina fiddled with the remote controls on

her bed until she discovered how to turn on the soft light. Then she reached for the top card. With shaking hands, she tore open the small white envelope. Although the words were written in Melanie's handwriting, it didn't take her long to realize the card was from Parker.

This is probably one of the hardest letters I've ever had to write. I don't know how to say this, because I know that words won't make the situation better, but I'm sorry about your accident. I'd give everything to make the world a fairer place for you to live in, but this time all I can do is tell you that I will help you in any way I can.

The only thing I do want you to know is that you are an awesome jockey and that I know you're going to find a way back to the track, because that is where you belong. You and Star are amazing together, and I know that this wasn't your last race.

Get some rest now. By the time you wake up again, I should be on a plane back to Kentucky. I'll be up in New York soon, though, and when I get there, I'll do anything I can to help you feel better.

Love, Parker

P.S. Hang in there. You'll always be a champion in my heart.

Christina smiled as she put Parker's card on the table. She knew her boyfriend had put a lot of thought into those words. She couldn't wait to see Parker again. But she couldn't believe that he would be spending his time comforting her rather than watching her and Star race in the Gold Cup.

Not wanting to slip back into feeling sorry for herself, Christina reached for the second card. As she opened it, she had to close her eyes several times when the throbbing in her ankle became more insistent. The pain seemed to multiply, ramping up to an almost unbearable intensity. *How am I ever going to ride again if it hurts this much now?* Christina wondered as tears of pain trickled down her already tear-stained cheeks. She could only imagine how much pain she would be in once she started riding. What if her ankle didn't heal?

Christina finally managed to get the card out of the envelope. She stared intently at the words, written in her mother's handwriting.

Dear Christina,

We know that you have a long road ahead of you, but we want you to know that your family will support you no matter what decisions you make.

Love always,

Mom, Dad, Mel, and Star

P.S. Star insisted that we give you a present. Look for it under your pillow.

Curious, Christina felt around under her pillow. Her hands brushed against a small box. Undoing the simple bow that held the box together, she opened the top to reveal a silver necklace with a small charm.

Tears filled Christina's eyes as she examined the flower charm. It was a carnation. On the day Star had won the Belmont, he had worn a blanket of carnations on his back.

Christina fell back against her pillow, gripping the necklace and crying. As the tears rolled down her face, Christina made a promise to herself. Her dreams for herself and Star weren't going to end at Belmont.

Christina's eyelids were getting heavy. She could feel herself drifting back to sleep, where the pain in her ankle would stop bothering her. The last thing she remembered thinking before falling asleep was, *No matter what it takes, Star and I are going to be a team again.*

4

"Are you sure you don't want to fly back to Kentucky?" Ashleigh asked for the third time that morning.

"Yes, Mom," Christina replied, shifting uncomfortably in the wheelchair. Despite her claims that she could handle crutches, her doctors had insisted that she use a wheelchair for at least the first week that she was out of the hospital. "I know I can't do much, but I want to stay with Star."

"I've talked with Samantha, and she's perfectly fine with you staying with her. With her pregnancy, she could probably use your help with her lessons," Ashleigh said. She packed the last of the items on the table beside Christina's bed.

Christina sighed as she wheeled her way toward the door of the hospital room. When she had woken up the previous morning, she had felt somewhat cheered by the promises she had made to herself the night before. She had apologized to her parents and Melanie and had put on a brave face despite the persistent pain in her ankle. That afternoon she had been further cheered by the news that the swelling in her ankle had subsided enough for them to remove the temporary splint and apply a cast the next day, which would allow her to leave the hospital. Now all she had to do was convince her mother that she would be all right at the track.

"When you've been injured before, Mom, did you stay away from the track?" Christina asked, already knowing the answer.

Ashleigh smiled, shaking her head. "I guess this is one of the times when I wish you would do as I say, not as I do." She zipped up the small suitcase. "I just think it would be easier for you to recover away from Belmont."

"We're all going home in a week anyway," Christina pointed out. "And Mel and I are moving to a handicapped-accessible room. It'll probably be easier for me to do the everyday things there than in my room at home or at Samantha's." Christina quickly looked around the hospital room to make sure she wasn't forgetting anything. She was eager to leave. The pink walls with their white trim were driving her crazy, as were the restrictions on her movements. "Besides, you know that I'm not going to abandon Star. We are stopping by the track to see him, aren't we?"

"Are you sure you don't want to go to your hotel room and lie down?"

"I've been lying down for the past three days," Christina replied. "I want to see my horse."

By the time Christina reached Belmont an hour later, she was questioning her eagerness to get to the track. Every bump of the car ride had jarred her ankle uncomfortably, especially as the last pain injection she had received at the hospital wore off. The doctor had given her some prescription pain medication, but Christina hadn't wanted to take any in case it gave her mom an excuse to make her go back to the hotel.

At the beginning of the car ride Christina had tried to distract herself by talking with her mother about Star's recent workouts. Melanie had been galloping her colt, and so far his times were rather lackluster. By the time they pulled off the highway toward the track, though, it was all Christina could do to grit her teeth through the bumps. After staying in bed for three days, the mere effort of sitting and holding her leg steady was exhausting.

Mike and Melanie were standing in the parking lot as Ashleigh pulled the car into one of the handicapped parking spots. Melanie opened Christina's wheelchair and held it while Mike and Ashleigh helped their daughter into it. Christina looked around during this transfer, hoping that no one was watching. She didn't want anyone to feel sorry for her.

Christina started to wheel herself toward the barns, but

her father insisted on pushing the chair. She was too tired to argue. "I'll just save my energy for Star," she mumbled to herself, vowing that the next day she would prove that she could handle most things on her own.

When they finally reached Star's stall, Christina's parents left her and Melanie alone with the colt. Star nickered when he saw Christina, then lowered his head to nose the wheelchair's armrest. Christina stroked the colt's head, rubbing the white star on his forehead. "I know, boy. I don't like this wheelchair, either. But just because I won't be riding doesn't mean that you're going to miss out on the big races. Melanie here is going to jockey you to the top."

"I hope so, Chris," Melanie said. "But I don't know if anyone other than you can bring out the best in him. With me, he doesn't seem to have that extra spark—the speed that made me scared to run Image against him in the Kentucky Derby."

"He's just confused by all the rider changes," Christina said, hoping that was true. She ran a hand down Star's sleek neck. "I'll go down to the track with you tomorrow and see if I can give you a hand with him."

"Hey, Christina!" Cindy called as she came down the barn aisle. "How are you feeling?" She gave Christina a hug and looked down at the cast that encased Christina's entire leg.

Christina shrugged. For a brief moment at Star's stall she had managed to forget the pain, but Cindy's question drew her attention back to the sharp throbbing. "I'm doing okay. It's good to be out of the hospital. Now I just have to find a way to ride again."

"I remember when I hurt my shoulder for the first time," Cindy said. "I was about your age, and all I could think about was what I could do to ride." Cindy put a hand on Christina's shoulder, getting her attention. "I want you to be careful with your recovery, Chris. Sometimes I think that if I hadn't pushed myself so hard each time I hurt my shoulder, I would still be riding."

"But how am I going to get back to the track if I don't push myself?"

"I'm not saying you shouldn't work hard," Cindy replied. "Just listen to your body. Don't ignore the pain. It's easy to—" Cindy stopped in midsentence as her cell phone rang. She quickly pulled the phone out of its belt clip. "I'm sorry, girls, but I have to take this. I'll see you later." With that, Cindy hurried down the aisle, leaving Christina and Melanie to wonder what was going on.

For almost every day of the past two years, Christina had gotten up at four-thirty each morning, put on her riding clothes, and exercised racehorses. This morning marked the beginning of a different routine.

Christina had set her alarm clock for a half hour earlier so that she could make it to the track when the workouts started. In retrospect, she probably could have used at least an extra hour. Everything took two or three times as long with her injury. It had taken her twenty minutes just to get all the waterproof wrappings around her cast so that she could take a shower. Getting dressed was also a struggle. Her parents had bought her several pairs of loose-fitting sweatpants and had cut away part of the left pant leg. Despite these attempts to make things easier, she still needed assistance.

But at last Christina parked her wheelchair in the front row of seats at the track, resigned to watching the morning workouts rather than riding in them. Several trainers and jockeys came up to her, briefly offering their best wishes, but for the most part people were too busy to notice her.

"Are you doing okay up there?" Melanie asked as she walked up to the outside rail after working Jinx. She took off her helmet and leaned against the railing casually.

"Yeah, I'm having loads of fun," Christina replied. Then, regretting her sarcasm, she softened her tone. "You and Jinx were fun to watch. He looks ready for the Futurity Stakes."

"I hope so," Melanie said, looking up the track to where Joe, one of Whitebrook's grooms, was leading her horse off the track. "He's so inconsistent. One day he's a perfect gentleman. The next day he's just all over the place." Melanie turned back to face Christina. "Anyway, Joe's going to bring Star out next. Any advice?"

Christina had prepared and revised a list of instructions while she'd been watching the horses work. "Star's gotten to a point where he doesn't like it when you expect him to be bad during a workout. If you're too hard on his mouth or if you use the crop too much, he rebels."

"That's pretty much the opposite of Jinx, where I have to anticipate any opportunity he has to misbehave."

"Sort of. If you have to get after Star to do something, treat it like a compromise. Do the usual things. Praise him when he does what you want, and make him do something again if he does it incorrectly. But if you get firm too fast, he'll do the exact opposite of what you want."

"You make him sound like a bratty teenager," Melanie said with a laugh.

Christina smiled, a grin that grew wider when Joe led Star up to her. "Yeah, he might be a bit of a brat sometimes, but he's my brat. And he knows I love him." She reached forward to pat Star's neck. "You be good for Melanie, okay?"

Christina's enthusiasm waned as she watched Star warm up. To her sensitive eyes, it seemed as though there was a little less spring in her colt's stride.

After they circled the track at a canter, Melanie asked Star for a gallop. The colt hesitated for a moment before changing gaits. Again, this seemed like a bad sign to Christina. It had been a long time since Star had balked at being asked to gallop.

When she and Star rounded the far turn, Melanie crouched lower over the colt's neck and asked him for speed.

"Go, Star!" Christina yelled.

41

For a moment Star almost seemed to slow. Melanie flicked the crop at him, and he began to run. As Melanie and Star came down the homestretch, Christina was certain that something wasn't working. Star, like many of Wonder's offspring, had always had an extra gear. When Cindy had worked with Star's older brother, Wonder's Champion, she had called it the "superdrive."

When Christina was riding, Star always went into his superdrive at the end of the breeze. But today he didn't get anywhere close.

Melanie's eyes were hooded with frustration as she rode Star back to the outside rail. Mike came over to meet her so that Christina would be able to hear the conversation.

"What was our time?" Melanie asked flatly.

"It's not as bad as you think." Mike showed Melanie and then Christina the stopwatch. "Maybe he's just saving his energy for the race."

Melanie shook her head. "I've seen Star go faster when Christina was galloping him on the trails."

"Don't worry so much," Mike said. "We had some more rain last night, so this might just be a case of him not liking the track. I know he'll perk up by race day."

But what if he doesn't? Christina asked silently as Mike and Melanie discussed their plans for Star's breeze the following day. She had several answers to her own question, none of which she liked.

• • •

The insistent tones of her cell phone woke Christina from a midafternoon nap. Struggling to open her eyes, she fumbled for the right button to answer the call. "Hello?" she said groggily.

"Hey, Chris. Guess who?"

Christina smiled. "Hi, Parker. Are you back in Kentucky?"

"Yeah, I'm calling from Whisperwood. I just got Foxy, Ozzie, and Black Hawke settled. How are you?"

Christina shifted her cast uncomfortably on the pile of pillows. Her doctor had instructed her to elevate her leg whenever possible to keep down the swelling. "I'm okay," she replied. "It's just hard to be watching Star rather than riding him."

"I'm sorry, sweetie," Parker said. "Anything I can do?"

"Not really. Just hurry up and get here." Christina shifted her cast again. When she had returned to her hotel room, she had taken a pain tablet in the hope that her ankle would stop bothering her. The medicine had put her to sleep. Now that she was awake, the throbbing had resumed, although at a decreased intensity. "I can't wait to see you."

"I can't wait to see you, either," Parker said. "Do you have a pen handy so I can give you my flight info?"

Christina reached for the pen and pad by the phone. "Yeah, I'm ready." She smiled as she copied down the flight numbers and times. Parker would be there in just three days.

"So how is Star doing?" Parker asked.

Christina sighed and told Parker about the morning workout. "He doesn't look like the same horse who won the Belmont."

"Maybe it's just the layoff," Parker pointed out. "This is the longest he's gone without racing since he got sick last year."

"I think it's more than that," Christina said. "Star and Melanie aren't clicking the way they need to in a race. But I can't think of any other jockey who would be better for him." Christina pounded the bed in frustration. "Why did I have to get injured? I'd give anything to be able to ride Star right now."

Christina knew Parker was staying quiet because he didn't know what to tell her. Not wanting him to feel sorry for her, she said, "I'm trying to stay positive. I figure that if I can do everything right with my recovery, I can be riding again at the beginning of Star's four-year-old season. That will give us another year to show the world what we can do."

Parker still didn't speak.

"What's wrong?" Christina asked.

"Um, you probably don't want to hear this, Chris, but I don't think it's a good idea for you to think too far ahead like that."

"Why not?" Christina demanded. "You've always told me to set goals."

"And you usually meet the goals you set," Parker said.

"I just don't want you to rush things this time because I'm worried about what it would mean for you later."

"What about Star? Am I supposed to let him down?"

"That's not what I'm saying, Chris. I want you to keep your hopes up, and I want you to ride Star as soon as you can. I just want to make sure that you're taking care of yourself."

Christina didn't like what Parker was saying, but she bit back an angry retort. She didn't want to take out her frustration on Parker, not when he was so worried about her. "Why are we talking about this? It's going to be months before I can even think about riding," Christina said. "Tell me how things have been going for you."

For the next ten minutes Parker had Christina giggling with stories about Ozzie's antics during the horse's final days in England. Ozzie had once been a champion jumper, but he had burned out on that circuit, eventually refusing to jump even the simplest fences. Parker had managed to retrain Ozzie to the point where the horse was becoming a decent eventer, but the horse was as erratic as Jinx. On his last day in England Ozzie had jumped a paddock fence. It had taken Parker and his friend Fiona two hours to find him. As it turned out, Ozzie had simply sneaked into a neighboring paddock and fallen asleep under a large tree.

"I should probably get going, Parker," Christina said when Parker had finished that story. "Cindy's invited us all out for a fancy dinner, and it's going to take me forever to get ready."

"Okay, Chris. I miss you. See you really soon." Parker made a kissing noise over the phone.

Christina smiled and air-kissed Parker back. "See you soon. I love you."

After hanging up the phone, Christina lay in bed for a long moment, thinking about what Parker had told her about not looking too far ahead. She had a feeling that everyone was going to give her the same advice. How was she going to convince them that she alone was capable of judging what she needed to do?

Cindy tapped her wineglass with her fork to get the table's attention. "I have an important announcement."

Christina stopped in midsentence. She and Melanie had been speculating about why Cindy had invited everyone to one of the nicer Italian restaurants in the area for dinner. Melanie had suggested that perhaps Cindy and Ben were getting engaged. Christina didn't think that was the case. Cindy and Ben certainly didn't seem to be acting any differently toward each other during the meal.

"Now, I know many of you have noticed that I've been distracted lately," Cindy began. "And I think it's time for me to tell you why." Cindy looked to her left, where her father was sitting. "I've always been so grateful to Ian and Beth for adopting me. They had no reason to take me in. I

46

was just a twelve-year-old runaway foster child who decided to sleep in a Whitebrook barn for the night. Ian and Beth gave me a family, and since I came back to Kentucky, I've wanted to do the same for someone else. Well, now I have that chance."

Melanie and Christina exchanged curious glances, but the other people at the table—Ben, Ashleigh, Mike, and Ian—began to smile.

"As all of you know, jockey Craig Avery died in a track accident at the end of the Saratoga meet. Two years before, his wife, Jilly Gordon, lost her fight with leukemia."

Christina looked down at the floor, feeling a lump rise in her throat. Craig and Jilly had both been friends of her mother's. Jilly had been Wonder's first jockey, riding the horse to victory in the Kentucky Derby. Ashleigh and Jilly had lost touch for a while when Jilly and Craig moved to California, but her mother had flown out to see Jilly several times before her death.

"Jilly and Craig had a fourteen-year-old daughter, Allison. Neither of them had any other family, so Allie was placed into temporary foster care. Since then, the Jockey Guild has been working to find a stable home for Allie." Cindy again looked at her adoptive father. "When I heard about this effort, I knew what I wanted to do. Luckily, Ian and Beth's stories about the volumes of red tape they had to cut through during my adoption prepared me for what I would face. They've both helped me so much with the process, as have Ashleigh and Ben, who both were great character and employment references." Cindy made eye contact with each person as she said his or her name. "It's taken a ton of meetings, phone calls, and paperwork, but today the social worker told me that Allie was going to be placed in my custody temporarily."

Everyone began to clap and cheer. Christina turned to her mother. "This is amazing. Why didn't Cindy tell us earlier?"

"She wanted to, but she was scared that her application wouldn't go through," Ashleigh whispered back. "She still remembers how hard it was for Ian and Beth to adopt her. The process took over a year."

"So when is Allie coming?" Ian asked.

"Her flight gets in Friday morning," Cindy answered. "After the Gold Cup, we'll fly back to Tall Oaks on Monday to help her get settled in."

"I'm proud of you, Cindy," Ian said. He raised his wineglass. "To Cindy, for making such a caring and selfless commitment."

Everyone raised their glasses. "To Cindy."

5

"IF YOU EVER WANTED TO SURPRISE ME, STAR, NOW WOULD be a good time," Christina mumbled as she wheeled herself closer to the rail. It was Thursday, time for Star's last breeze before the Gold Cup.

Christina herself was sorely in need of some good news. The day before, Star had turned in one of his worst times of the year. Then during the afternoon she'd gone to see Dr. Renkovic, an orthopedist Cindy had recommended, to get a timetable for her recovery. Dr. Renkovic had warned Christina that it was still far too early to set any firm dates. However, the current estimates were that her leg would need to stay in a cast until late November, and there wasn't anything she could do in the way of rehabilitation before then.

As Melanie prepared for the breeze, Christina crossed her fingers, hoping her cousin would get through to Star and convince him to run his best. Star leaped into a brisk gallop, but it was obvious even from his first strides that nothing had changed. The colt ran at a fast pace, but he never clicked into top gear. Even when Melanie resorted to the crop, Star responded with only a slight increase in pace.

"I know you must be disappointed," Ashleigh said to her daughter as they watched.

"It's just that Star was training so well before I got hurt," Christina replied. "I know Mel's trying. She keeps asking me what she could do better, and I've given her all the advice I can think of." Christina turned her chair so that she could see her colt. "I want to believe that Dad's right about Star just not liking the track, but I think it's more than that."

"Star does have a history of disliking muddy tracks." Ashleigh checked her stopwatch and wrote Star's time on her clipboard.

"Maybe we should scratch him," Christina blurted out. The thought had been floating in her head since Star's first lackluster workout, but she had been afraid to voice it. "I don't think it would be good for him to lose a race after such a long layoff."

"What if the long layoff is the problem?" Ashleigh argued. "From February to June Star ran in about one race a month. We had to keep him sharp all the time in preparation for the next race. Maybe he's just forgotten what it's like to have to run against other horses, and being in a race again will remind him."

Christina was silent as she considered her mother's words.

"Star is your horse, Chris. So it's your choice. But personally, I'd be very wary of running him in a big race like the Classic without preparation."

Christina nodded slowly. Her mother was right.

Before Christina could say anything, Melanie and Star came over to her. "Sorry, Chris. It's just like last time," Melanie said. "I couldn't get through to him." Melanie shook her head, clearly unhappy with her ride.

"It's all right, Mel," Christina replied. "Mom and I have been discussing it, and we're thinking that maybe a little competition will remind Star of why he needs to run. He's going to have that in just a couple of days."

"Yeah, he will," Melanie agreed. She patted Star's neck. "And once he sees Celtic Mist blowing past him, Star won't have any choice but to kick into his superdrive, right?"

Christina nodded halfheartedly. Celtic Mist was Townsend Acres' best three-year-old. The colt had beaten Star in both the Kentucky Derby and the Preakness, and he had recently won the Travers Stakes. For Star's sake, Christina hoped her mother and Melanie were right.

"Easy, Jinx, easy. I know it's crazy out here, but you need to calm down." Christina reached up to stroke the big chest-

51

nut, but Jinx would have none of that. He tossed his head and shied sideways. Joe had to jump out of the way to avoid being kicked.

"We could really use Mel right now," Mike murmured through gritted teeth as he tightened the girth. "She's the only one who can calm him down when he's like this."

Melanie, of course, was in the jockeys' lounge. One of the track's rules was that all riders had to be in the jockeys' lounge before the start of the first race on the card, and they couldn't leave until after they rode their last race of the day.

"Do you want me to get Mom?" Christina asked, eager to do something.

"No, she's busy with March," Mike said, quickly fastening the girth. Whitebrook also had a two-year-old, March to Honor, entered in the Futurity Stakes.

March to Honor was the son of two of Whitebrook's champions, March to Glory and Honor Bright. This pairing had already produced one great horse, a filly named Honor and Glory, who had placed third in the Kentucky Derby. Christina knew her parents were hoping March would have the same sort of success, and so far, he had won two out of three races.

Farther down the aisle, Christina saw Brad Townsend looking over Light Fandango, the best of Townsend Acres' two-year-old prospects. Brad nodded at her curtly.

Christina had ridden Light Fandango to a second-place finish in the Kentucky Cup during the summer. It had been part of her way of paying to board Star at Townsend Acres.

Christina's parents and Brad had been rivals since before Christina was born, and for the first part of her stay at Townsend Acres, Christina had found herself wondering why her parents disliked him so much. However, when Brad had nearly manipulated things so that he would own Image, Christina had realized that no matter how polite and nice he was on the surface, Brad was always looking out for his own interest.

Since leaving Townsend Acres, Christina had spoken with Brad only a few times. Two days earlier he'd bumped into her in the barn aisle and wished her luck with her recovery. They had briefly discussed the Gold Cup, although it was clear that Brad didn't consider Star much of a threat without Christina riding.

With Parker coming to New York, Christina wondered whether she would see more of Brad. When father and son got together, it seemed as though they couldn't go for more than a few minutes without arguing. Christina was very thankful that Parker was so unlike his father.

"Chris, we're going to take Jinx out. You'd better get out of the way." Mike fastened the chin strap on the colt's racing bridle just as Jinx kicked out with his hind legs.

Christina nodded, wheeling herself to the side. She couldn't wait until she got back to Kentucky and could start using crutches. Now that all her other cuts and bruises from the accident were mostly healed, she was eager for the increased mobility.

Knowing that she would be no help in the walking

ring, Christina made her way slowly toward the stands. She turned back a couple of times as she left the saddling area. Once she saw Jinx try to rear, and the other time the colt tried to bite Joe's shoulder.

Despite her head start, Christina made it to the seats only a few minutes ahead of her parents. "How are the horses?" she asked when they arrived.

"March is fine, but Melanie's going to have a tough ride on Jinx," Ashleigh said. "It's a shame the colt picked today to have one of his moods."

"Yeah, he was so good yesterday. Maybe it's a good thing Jazz couldn't make it to the race," Christina replied. Jazz had originally planned on flying up to Belmont that morning, but he had called Melanie the day before to say that he had made other plans with the band. Melanie had been rather upset because she'd been hoping to have a long talk with her boyfriend about both their horses and their future as a couple.

"And they're off!" The announcer's voice broke through Christina's musings. She took her binoculars from her lap and focused on the pack of horses. Light Fandango had taken the lead. Despite her mixed feelings toward Townsend Acres, Christina liked the little bay. He had shown a lot of heart during the Kentucky Cup.

Christina scanned the rest of the horses, pausing when she saw Jinx. The big chestnut colt was already getting rank with Melanie, galloping unevenly and pulling at the reins. Melanie was trying to sit cool, but Christina knew from experience that it was probably taking all her strength just to hold her horse. Further back, March to Honor, a late closer, seemed to be moving comfortably.

"The time for the first quarter mile is a comfortable twenty-four seconds. Light Fandango holds a half-length lead over Trivial Pursuits. Hi Jinx has moved up to third."

Christina wasn't sure which horse to cheer. She knew her parents wanted March to win, although they would be happy for Mel if she pulled off a victory on Jinx. Personally, she also had to root for Light Fandango, who was running gamely despite the track conditions.

Christina focused on Melanie and Jinx again. The colt was still moving sideways. Melanie had to work hard just to ensure that Jinx didn't interfere with anyone else.

"Forty-six seconds for the half mile. Light Fandango still leads over Trivial Pursuits. Then it's High Jinx and Battleflag, followed by March to Honor." Christina missed having to strain above the sound of pounding hooves to hear the announcer's voice. In the stands, it was perfectly clear.

Christina put down her binoculars, wanting a view of the entire field. March was making his move. He passed Battleflag on the inside, then moved up to Jinx's flank.

Jinx, on the other hand, seemed to be struggling. Melanie had given her colt his head, but he wasn't moving the way Christina knew he could. In the Kentucky Cup, Jinx had blown past Light Fandango when Melanie had stopped holding her horse back. Now he seemed more intent on careening toward the rail.

Light Fandango was maintaining the lead. Meanwhile, March was running easily alongside Jinx, a length back. Ashleigh had instructed March's jockey, Dave Randall, not to let the colt run full out until the very end.

As the horses rounded the far turn, Light Fandango dug in and sped up. But the other horses were ready. Trivial Pursuits dropped back, but Jinx and March surged forward, almost pulling even. Melanie had been forced to take Jinx wide so that her colt wouldn't hit any of the other horses, and this gave March the advantage as the horses headed toward the homestretch.

"Come on! Go! Go!" Christina was careful not to name any horses as she cheered. From where she stood, though, she guessed that it would be March's race unless Melanie found a way to make Jinx focus.

She was right. March to Honor crossed the finish line three-quarters of a length ahead of a tiring Light Fandango. Jinx finished fourth.

Instead of joining her parents in the winner's circle, Christina headed back to the barn to talk with her cousin. While she waited for Melanie, she visited with Charisma. The filly was recovering well from her injuries. Most of the deeper cuts on her left side and neck had closed, and the vet was confident there would be minimal scarring. Melanie was planning on taking her out on the track the next day, and Ashleigh would be making a decision soon about whether to run Charisma in the Breeders' Cup Juvenile Fillies. Christina hoped her mother would go for it. It was bad enough that the accident had left her unable to ride. She didn't want it to affect Charisma as well.

As Christina stroked Charisma's forehead, she looked over the scars on the filly's neck. "Are you going to be scared when you get back on the track?" Christina asked the filly. "Do you think Halo Delight will be?" Halo Delight had come out of the accident with several bone chips and would be sidelined for about six months. "At least you don't have to see videos of the accident." Christina had tried watching the race tape only once. Seeing herself dragged across the track and bouncing like a rag doll had made her sick to her stomach.

"Hey, Chris. You should be joining the party at March's stall." At the sound of Melanie's glum voice, Christina turned away from Charisma. Melanie was leading a more subdued Jinx with Joe following behind in case she needed backup.

"I thought you might want someone to talk to," Christina replied. "But if you want to be alone, I can go find Mom and Dad."

Melanie shrugged. "Jinx is just doing the on again, off again thing. One day he acts like a horse who could break track records. The next he's almost as bad as he was the day I bought him. We need to get more consistency before racing him again. He could have caused an accident out there today." Melanie let Jinx into his stall. The colt gave a tired nicker as he stepped inside. "Of course, Jazz probably won't go along with giving him time."

"Have you told him about the race?" Christina asked.

Melanie shook her head. "He's going to be upset. He might even bring up the idea of selling Jinx again. I'm not ready for that conversation." Melanie leaned against Jinx's stall. "I don't know what's happening to Jazz. At first he was so excited about buying another racehorse for me to work with. Then when things didn't go the way he expected in Europe, he became this completely different person. I mean, right now I don't even know if I want to be with him anymore."

Christina wheeled herself closer to Melanie, trying to think of a suitable reply. She had noticed the friction between Melanie and Jazz, but she had assumed that Jazz would eventually stop being so unreasonable.

"I keep asking Jazz to come to Kentucky to visit," Melanie continued. "That way he could at least see the horses. But he says he can't leave the band right now."

"Any chance you could go down to Florida anzd talk to him?" Christina suggested.

"Not right now. I need to ride in all the races I can to put some money away. I'm hoping that if I take care of some of Jinx's bills, Jazz won't complain as much." Melanie let herself into Jinx's stall and ran her hands down the colt's legs, checking them for swelling or heat. "Besides, if everyone else in the band is in as bad a mood as he is, I don't think I'd enjoy being there. I just hope I can find a way to get through to Jinx before his next race."

Christina remained silent while Melanie finished examining Jinx. She, too, hoped that Jinx would become more consistent. But she knew that sometimes only time would make that happen. And time was something that Melanie probably wouldn't get.

6

"HAVE A GOOD DAY!" CINDY CALLED AS SHE PULLED OUT OF the parking space.

Christina waved as Cindy drove away. Cindy had volunteered to drop Christina off at Starting Line Equine Hospital on her way to the airport to pick up Allie. Christina had made her first trip to this equine surgery clinic in June. Callie had been moved here after his accident, and his unsuccessful operation had taken place in the main surgical suite.

In the wake of Callie's death, Cindy had introduced Christina to Dr. John Reuter, one of the three veterinarians at the facility. Dr. Reuter had talked with Christina about her goal of becoming a vet, and Christina had kept in touch with him via e-mail since the summer. When Dr. Reuter heard

Christina was returning to Belmont, he had offered to let her spend a day at the clinic with him.

Dr. Reuter was talking with an anxious owner in the waiting room when Christina entered. She sat quietly, ignoring the curious stares from the receptionists. In the past few days she had gotten tired of telling people what had happened to her ankle.

"Hi, Christina. I'm glad you could make it," Dr. Reuter said. "You ready to learn more about how we do things around here?"

Christina nodded, looking up at the tall blond-haired doctor. "Thanks so much for letting me do this."

"No problem. Now, I figure that you're probably sick of people asking about your ankle. So I'm going to assume that you aren't having any trouble unless you tell me otherwise, all right?"

Christina nodded again, glad Dr. Reuter understood. "Where are we going first?"

"I need to finish checking on the horses in the recovery stalls before my first surgery at ten," Dr. Reuter replied. "Why don't you help me?"

Although Christina wasn't sure she would be much help, she followed Dr. Reuter down a hallway to the back of the clinic. The clinic was one of the largest, most impressive facilities she had ever seen. Off just this one hallway, there was an ultrasound room and an X-ray suite.

The recovery stalls were in an extension at the back of the building. The stalls were roomy and padded. Two veterinary technicians were on duty at all times, and they checked the horses hourly. Beyond the stalls, there was an outdoor exercise pool and several acres of grassy paddocks.

"How long did it take for Starting Line to expand like this?" Christina asked. She had watched Image rehabilitate at Brad's spacious veterinary facility, but even that was nothing compared to this clinic. If she became a vet, she wanted everything to run as efficiently as things did here, without losing the personal touch.

"Well, we're constantly building, reassessing, and then building some more," Dr. Reuter answered. "In the ten years since I've been here, we've built a dozen new recovery stalls, brought in the ultrasound equipment, and added a second surgical suite." Dr. Reuter paused at the stall of a small jet-black horse and picked up a chart. "This filly was injured in a freak accident in the paddock." He took out a pen and began writing as he talked. "It's a shame. She was running, stepped into a rabbit hole, and broke her cannon bone. Her owners had such high hopes for her. They told me she has three Triple Crown winners in her bloodlines: Whirlaway, Secretariat, and Affirmed."

Christina had seen enough amazing horses come out of nowhere to know that bloodlines didn't necessarily mean anything on the track. The best horses didn't necessarily pass their talent on to their offspring. However, when buying yearlings, owners often had little more than conformation and bloodlines to go on. "Are they still planning to race her?"

"I doubt it. This type of injury is associated with poor outcomes when the leg is stressed. But she's going to be a beautiful broodmare."

Christina studied the black filly carefully. The horse did have straight legs, a long neck, and a nicely sculpted head. There was also a glint in the filly's eye that reminded Christina of another injured horse: Image. "What's her name?" Christina wondered as she reached up, letting the filly sniff her hand.

"Tilt-a-Whirl. The owners really wanted to play off Whirlaway, I guess."

Christina knew a little about Whirlaway, who had won the Triple Crown in the 1940s. The chestnut horse had apparently had some rather dangerous behaviors, the kind that might have enticed a daredevil jockey like Melanie. Whirlaway's trainer had switched jockeys just before the Triple Crown, finding Eddie Arcaro, who was known for his even demeanor. Christina only wished that switching jockeys always gave such good results.

"We actually have two descendants of Whirlaway here right now," Dr. Reuter said as he continued down the aisle. This time he stopped by the stall of a bay colt. "This is Victory Runaway. He's a two-year-old by Victory Gallop and out of a mare with Whirlaway bloodlines."

Christina could remember Victory Gallop's Triple Crown races. The horse had spoiled a Triple Crown bid for Real Quiet in 1998, winning the Belmont by a nose. Victory Gallop's trainer had changed jockeys between Triple

Crown races. Gary Stevens, who had narrowly missed winning the Triple Crown the year before with Silver Charm, had gotten the mount.

Other famous horses have had different jockeys and been fine. Actually, most horses don't have the same rider for every race. I would have ridden Star for the rest of his career if I could, but now that I can't, how am I going to teach him to accept Melanie? Christina shook her head, pushing back those thoughts. Dr. Reuter was generously offering to show her around, and he deserved her attention. "Why is he here?" she asked as Victory Runaway explored her wheelchair with his nose.

"We had to operate because of a twisted intestine. He's lucky that we caught it early," Dr. Reuter replied. The vet peered over the door of the adjacent stall, where a veterinary technician was changing another horse's bandage. "When you're done with that, can you feed Runaway a bit of bran mash?" he asked the tech. "I've checked his temp, and it's normal."

Christina gently pushed Runaway's muzzle away from her chair. "You're going to get fed soon enough," she teased. "Why would you want to eat my chair?"

Dr. Reuter laughed. "You know, you're the first person Runaway hasn't shied away from here," he remarked.

Christina shrugged. "My friend Samantha, who used to run a therapeutic riding program, once told me that she thought horses could sense when someone was vulnerable, and they would act differently around that person. Since I got hurt, even Star seems to know that he has to be gentle."

"How long will it be before you can ride again?" Dr. Reuter walked to the last stall in the aisle, where a gray mare was recovering.

"No one's sure yet. The earliest estimate I've been given so far is six months, but I hope to make it sooner." Christina watched as the mare took a tentative step forward. Her right leg was encased in a protective boot.

"Would you be interested in a job while you're waiting?" Dr. Reuter asked.

Christina looked up at the vet, surprised. "What kind of job?"

"I'm working with some vets in Kentucky and California to study the differences between surgical and therapeutic interventions for racehorses with suspensory ligament tears," Dr. Reuter replied. "Basically, owners of injured racehorses who come to one of our clinics will have the opportunity to enroll in the trial, and the horses will be randomized to receive either surgery or therapy. Horses will be followed for one year to examine recovery time, racetrack performance, and reinjury rate." Dr. Reuter gestured to the horse in the stall. "Gray Wind here is one of the first horses in our surgical group. For the next year we're going to take ultrasounds of her leg once a month. Also, when she starts healing, we'll look at parameters such as her range of motion." Dr. Reuter ran a hand down the mare's back. "Anyway, there's going to be a lot of data to crunch. Would you like to be involved?"

Analyzing data wasn't exactly Christina's idea of the

perfect job, but many veterinarians did some sort of research, and perhaps this would be a good way to get some exposure to that field. She certainly wouldn't be up to working with horses in any other setting for a while. "Sure. I think it could be interesting," Christina said, trying to sound eager.

"I'm not saying it's going to be exciting," Dr. Reuter warned her. "I was never much of a numbers person. But Dr. Dietrich has a great clinic down in Kentucky, and I'm sure she and her partner will be glad to have you. When I tell her about you, I'll also make sure that she lets you see the clinic beyond the computer."

"I'd like that," Christina said, smiling. She was glad she would have something to do once she got back to Kentucky.

Dr. Reuter looked at his watch. "My first surgery's in twenty minutes, so I'd better get ready. Are you still interested in watching?"

The last time Christina had been in that operating room, she had nearly passed out because all she could think about was Callie's death. But even though she still had nightmares about that accident, she was ready to move on. "Yes," she replied. "Let's go."

It was past five when Christina returned to her motel room. For the first part of the drive back she had talked nonstop with Melanie about what she had seen. In the space of six hours, Dr. Reuter had performed three scheduled surgeries as well as an emergency colic surgery. The scheduled surgeries had included a suspensory ligament operation for the study, a gelding procedure, and a bone chip removal.

"I don't think I would have been able to keep my lunch down if I'd seen a horse's intestines laid out on a table," Melanie had said, looking both intrigued and horrified. "But it sounds like you had a better afternoon than I did."

"How did your races go?"

"Well, in the first race I was moved down from second to third because my mount bumped another horse. Then in the third, the Dreamflight colt I was on decided that nothing I could do to him was going to make him run. And after those two losses, Jazz called."

Christina saw her cousin tense up. Jazz had not returned Melanie's calls the previous day. "What did he want?"

"He says that we're going to run Jinx again within the next month whether I think he's ready or not. I'm trying to find a race at Lone Star Park so that I can bring Jinx down with all Whitebrook's Breeders' Cup prospects." Melanie sighed. "As much as I hate to say this, I'm starting to wish that I could get a loan and try to buy Jinx from Jazz." Melanie shook her head. "But that's just wishful thinking. Tell me more about the Whirlaway descendants. Maybe I can think positively and hope Jinx will be able to overcome his problems and do as well as Whirlaway did during his three-year-old year."

For the rest of the ride Melanie kept the conversation on

Christina's day. When they were back at the motel, Melanie gently teased Christina as she helped her get ready for her date with Parker.

Christina got ready as fast as she could in a wheelchair. She wanted to look her best since she hadn't seen her boyfriend in three months.

"Christina, I think there's someone at the door for you," Melanie said, her eye to the peephole, just as Christina finished putting on her makeup. "Either that, or Parker's decided to drown me in roses."

If she'd been able to, Christina would have jumped out of her chair in excitement. Instead, she asked Melanie to open the door, and she wheeled herself into the doorway.

The moment the door opened, Parker immediately went to Christina's side. His smoky gray eyes widened as he looked at her. "You're beautiful," he said softly. He kissed her on the cheek, then on the lips. "I've missed you."

Christina pulled Parker close, burying her face in his shoulder and enjoying his familiar scent. "I've missed you, too."

Melanie made gagging noises. "I've changed my mind, Chris. Seeing a horse's guts spread out on a table doesn't make me sick. This does."

"Sorry, Mel," Parker said, grinning. He pulled away, although he still held Christina's hand.

"No worries," Melanie replied. "Before you two love-birds go have your dinner, do you want to come with me to Cindy's room to meet Allie?"

68

"Of course," Christina and Parker said in unison.

Melanie took the half dozen red roses from Christina's lap. "Do you want me to put these in water for you?"

"Yeah, thanks." Christina squeezed Parker's hand, then reluctantly let go. She knew it must be hard for Melanie to see them together when things were so rocky between her and Jazz.

Parker started to push Christina down the hall but stopped when he saw the look on her face. Instead, he just walked by her side, keeping a hand on her shoulder as they made their way to Cindy's room.

Cindy answered the door after one knock. "Hey, Parker, welcome back. Christina, did you have a good day at the clinic?"

"Yeah, it was really interesting," Christina replied. She wheeled her chair into the room and saw a short, brown-haired girl sitting on the second bed. "Hi, Allie," she said. "I'm Christina Reese. I'd shake your hand, but it's a bit of an obstacle course in here." Cindy had never been known for her tidiness, and there were half-unpacked suitcases and racing magazines strewn on the floor.

Allie's plain facial features relaxed into a pretty smile. She stood up and walked over to Christina, shaking her hand. "It's nice to meet you," she said softly.

"Christina is the owner and jockey of Wonder's Star," Cindy added. "I'll introduce you to him at the track tomorrow."

"You'll probably have more fun meeting the horses

than the people," Christina joked, wanting to make Allie more comfortable. "They're easier. You don't have to talk, and they'll like you as long as you bring them carrots."

"Chris is right. Just stay away from my horse, Jinx. He either greets people by biting them or nudging them, and it's impossible to predict what he's going to do beforehand," Melanie said. "I'm Melanie, by the way."

"And I'm Parker. You won't be meeting any of my silly animals until you get back to Kentucky. And when you do, don't believe anything Cindy's sister, Samantha, says about me."

Allie smiled, though to Christina it looked a little forced.

"Allie has done some stadium jumping and eventing, Parker," Cindy said, crossing the room to stand next to her foster daughter. "I thought it would be fun for her to take lessons with you and Sam."

"That would be great. I promise not to be too mean, Allie," Parker said with a wink. Then he glanced at the clock on Cindy's nightstand.

Cindy followed Parker's gaze. "You and Chris had better hurry if you're going to make it for your reservation. I wouldn't want to ruin your first night together in months."

"We'll be okay," Christina said. "Where are we going, Parker?"

Parker smiled mysteriously. "I'd tell you, but then I'd have to kill you." He began walking toward the door. "It

70

was nice to meet you, Allie. I'll see you at the track tomorrow."

Christina noticed that Allie lowered her head when the track was mentioned. She tried to think of ways to distract Allie the next day. Of course, with Star racing in the Gold Cup, she'd need to be distracted herself. "See you tomorrow, Allie. It should be a good day of races."

"Have I told you how beautiful you look tonight?" Parker asked as they waited for the waiter to bring their food. Parker had taken Christina to a nice steak house, insisting they share a huge prime rib.

"Only about ten times," Christina replied with a smile. "But there are worse things you could repeat."

"I'm just glad to be back." Parker smiled. "And I hope I've come back in time to keep you from going stir-crazy here."

Christina sighed. "Everyone treats me like I'm fragile. Yesterday I had to beg Ian to let me clean tack! Only Dr. Reuter seems to understand that I'm the only one who really knows my limits."

"That's probably because he doesn't know the Christina I know—the one who is always challenging her limits."

"Maybe, but no one's given me any reason why I shouldn't, and it's not like I'm going to do something crazy

71

like race Star in the Gold Cup tomorrow." Christina took a long drink of water, trying to cool her frustrations.

"So how much of this stir-crazy thing has to do with your injury and how much has to do with Star?"

Christina shrugged. "They're the same thing. I'm injured, so I can't ride Star."

Parker reached across the table, taking Christina's hands to stop her from fidgeting. He gently traced circles in her palms with his thumbs. "Everything's going to be okay tomorrow."

"You haven't seen the way Star's been running."

"Maybe not," Parker conceded. "But I've never known Star to give up without a fight."

Christina smiled. Parker was right about that. "Anyway, I shouldn't ruin our night by worrying about the race. Tell me about what's going to happen in your meeting in New Jersey."

Parker tightened his grip on Christina's hands involuntarily. "Now you're making me nervous," he said. "Actually, I have no idea. I've tried talking with Lyssa, but even she doesn't have a clue." Parker's friendly rival Lyssa Hynde had been invited to join the United States Equestrian Team earlier that spring. "I figure that what happened at Burghley at least got their attention, but was it enough to overcome my hothead image?"

"In a few years they'll be glad to have a hothead like you on the Olympic team."

"Perhaps." Parker sighed. "I don't want to think about

that right now. Instead I want to plan what we're going to do when we get back to Kentucky. Since I'm going into light training to give my horses a break and you won't be riding, I figure we'll have plenty of time to take some day trips."

With that, Christina and Parker began tossing around some possible destinations. Christina knew that they wouldn't make it to some of them because of her ankle, but she was so happy that Parker was back that she was willing to indulge him. They would be worrying about their respective futures soon enough. For now, it would be nice just to enjoy the evening.

7

"GOOD MORNING, STAR," CHRISTINA SAID SOFTLY. SHE slowly made her way down the quiet barn aisle. Many of the horses were still dozing, and she heard very few stamps and nickers as she approached Star's stall.

It was so early in the morning that the sun was barely a hint of red and orange in the dawn sky. Instead of coming to the track with Melanie as usual, Christina had come out with her parents, who always arrived just before four-thirty.

Star had been dozing, but he woke when he heard Christina's voice, and whuffed softly into her hand. "Did you sleep well, boy? You probably had a better night than I did."

Christina had tossed and turned all night with both

worry and pain. Her ankle had given her some trouble, and she hadn't wanted to take any painkillers because she was afraid they would leave her mind fuzzy on race day.

"I thought the Belmont was going to be a new beginning for us," Christina continued. "We figured out so much together during the Triple Crown, and I just felt that as long as we were together, we weren't going to lose." Christina rested her head against Star's outstretched neck. "I know it's silly, but I dreamed that you would be Horse of the Year. I thought that if you won the Travers, the Gold Cup, and the Classic, there was no way the voters could overlook you. But what happens if you don't win another race this year? Celtic Mist would probably beat you out for the three-year-old colt Eclipse Award."

Christina ran a hand down Star's neck, resting it on his shoulder. "I know I'm lucky to have you and that awards don't matter. But this year is so important to me because I don't know what's going to happen now. When am I going to be able to ride you again? *Am* I going to be able to ride you again?"

Christina wheeled her chair closer to Star. "You know what's even worse?" she asked, lowering her voice. "The first time I saw Mel breeze you, I think some small part of me didn't want you to run well. I wanted to know that we had something special, that there was something I could bring out in you that no one else could." Christina buried her face in Star's coat. "That seems stupid, doesn't it? It's just like wanting to win an award. Why do I need the world to know what I already do?"

"Good morning, Christina." Cindy's cheerful voice was a counterpoint to Christina's darker mood.

Christina looked up and saw Allie trailing slightly behind Cindy. "Good morning, Cindy—hi, Allie. Is Gratis ready for the big race?" Christina knew that Gratis would be a horse to watch out for. He had placed in almost every race he'd been entered in that year.

"I hope so," Cindy replied. "Because Melanie wasn't available, I had a hard time picking another jockey. I ended up going with Aaron from Dreamflight."

"Wow. I'm sure Aaron was thrilled." Aaron Evans had become one of Christina's good friends when she'd raced Star in the Santa Anita Derby that spring. "I thought he was back in California. When did he get to New York?"

"Just yesterday. I guess the Johnstons called him because they needed someone to take over all your mounts. Aaron exercised Gratis a couple of times up at Saratoga, and they got along pretty well." Cindy turned to look at her foster daughter. "Anyway, we're probably boring Allie with all this talk of people and horses she doesn't know."

"No, not at all," Allie replied. She took a step closer to Star, holding her hand out so that the colt could sniff it. "Is it okay if I touch him?"

"Of course it is," Christina answered, rolling her chair back to give Allie some room. "Star usually likes meeting new people."

Star sniffed Allie's hand uncertainly a few times. Then, apparently deciding that she was okay, he nudged her shoulder. "Hey, boy," Allie said quietly. "I think you're the most handsome horse I've seen at the track."

"I agree," Christina said. "Actually, I could use some help making him more handsome before race day. Are you interested in a job, Allie?"

"Sure," Allie replied. "As long as it's okay with Cindy."

"Of course it's all right," Cindy said with a smile. "But I have to warn you, Christina will make you earn your pay."

"You don't have to pay me," Allie protested, looking surprised.

"Yes, I do. Just don't tell Parker, because he's doing free labor." As she spoke, Christina began to feel a bit better about the day. She hadn't liked the idea of having to ask her parents and the grooms at Whitebrook to do everything she thought needed to be done. It would be easier to work with Allie and Parker. "Anyway, would you mind giving Star a quick wake-up grooming?"

Allie nodded. She picked up a bucket of brushes and let herself into Star's stall.

"Thanks," Cindy whispered to Christina as Allie began running a currycomb down Star's back. The colt grunted and then nickered, clearly enjoying the grooming. "I wasn't sure what she was going to do all day while I was busy with Gratis."

"No problem," Christina replied. Later she would have

to tell Cindy that she needed the distraction of working with Allie as much as Allie probably needed the distraction of working with her.

"And they're off!" The track announcer's voice echoed through the nearly empty track cafeteria.

Christina glanced up at the television monitor, then looked back down at her sandwich. She lifted the slice of bread and took out some of the bell peppers.

"Do you want to bring our food to the stands and watch?" Parker suggested.

Christina shook her head. "I want to stay near Star." She carefully arranged the bell peppers on the edge of her plate.

"You know I'm not going to let you go back to Star's stall until you eat, right?" Parker continued. "And building a pepper tower doesn't qualify as eating."

Allie, who was sitting next to Parker, giggled. It was only the second time Christina had heard the young girl laugh all morning. The first had been when Parker had sprayed Allie with the hose while they were giving Star a bath.

Christina forced herself to take a bite of the sandwich. Her mouth was dry, making it difficult to chew. She had managed to distract herself all morning, throwing herself into getting Star ready for the race and trying to draw Allie into the easy banter between her and Parker. But now Star was resting in his stall, her parents were busy getting other

78

Whitebrook horses ready for the earlier races, and Melanie was in the jockeys' lounge.

The Jockey Club Gold Cup was the seventh and final race on the day's card. That gave Christina about five hours with absolutely nothing to do. She hadn't waited for one of Star's races outside the jockeys' lounge in over a year, and she didn't know how to pass the time.

"Are you all right, Chris?" Parker asked, sounding concerned.

"I'm okay," Christina replied quickly. "I just wish there were a pool table around here so that I could at least pretend I was hanging out with the other jockeys."

"What if I got some extra cups and we wadded our sandwich wrappers into balls? Then we could pretend we were bowling."

"The ball wouldn't be big enough," Allie pointed out. Like Christina, she had hardly touched her lunch.

Parker shrugged. "Well, you can't blame a guy for trying." He aimed his wadded sandwich wrapper at the trash can. "How about basketball?" His shot missed by two feet. "Guess that's out, too." Parker reached into his pocket for his keys. "Luckily, I have a backup surprise."

"What's that?" Christina asked.

Parker grinned mischievously. "I'll be back in a minute." He gave Christina a quick kiss on the cheek.

"What do you think he's up to?" Allie asked Christina as they watched Parker leave.

"I have no idea," Christina replied. "Parker's been like

this for as long as I've known him. You should have seen him a few years ago, right after he came back from boarding school in England. He had a reputation for being quite a troublemaker."

"Really?" Allie raised her eyebrows in surprise.

"Oh, don't let that innocent boyish grin fool you," Christina said. "He's been in his fair share of sticky situations. He actually was expelled from the boarding school in England because he stole a car—well, in his words, he borrowed it. I think he's good for me, though. He forces me to be more adventurous."

"That's how it was between my mom and dad," Allie said. She twisted her napkin in her hands, and Christina could see her knuckles turning white. "Dad used to take Mom rock climbing even though she was scared of heights. Even after Mom got sick—" Allie looked away. "He still took her on whitewater rafting trips." Allie began to shred the napkin methodically. She wouldn't make eye contact with Christina.

Christina was silent for a moment as she tried to think of the right thing to say. "You probably don't remember this, but my parents and I made a trip out to California to visit your parents when I was eight. Instead of doing the usual tourist activities, Craig took us camping in a national park."

"I've seen pictures of that," Allie said. "There's one of both of us standing on a big rock. Dad told me it took him forever to convince me I wasn't going to fall."

Christina saw Allie bite her lip. She reached across the table and put her hand on the girl's shoulder.

Allie quickly straightened. "I'm okay."

"So, what are you two girls gossiping about?" Parker asked. He walked across the cafeteria quickly, holding a large shopping bag.

"Just girl stuff," Christina replied, not wanting to embarrass Allie. "What have you got there?"

"Cover your eyes," Parker instructed. "You too, Allie."

Christina groaned, but she obediently put her hands over her eyes. She heard rustling as Parker opened the bag. Then there was a distinct thud as he dropped something onto the table.

"Okay, you can open your eyes now," Parker said. He gestured to the box in the middle of the table. It was a 250-piece jigsaw puzzle. The scene was of a horse running on the beach. "Five bucks says that you two can't finish this in the next two hours."

Christina looked at Allie. "You in?" she asked. When Allie nodded, she opened the box. "Okay, Parker. You're on."

Star tossed his head regally as Mike led him into the walking ring. Christina smiled as the high-spirited colt whinnied a challenge at the other horses.

A little while earlier Christina and Allie had won their bet with Parker, fitting the final blue-gray ocean pieces in the correct place by trial and error. Parker had accepted this

81

loss good-naturedly, joking that he would have the puzzle framed.

After that lighthearted challenge, it had been time for Star's race. Christina had stood by and watched while Parker, Mike, and Ashleigh readied Star in the saddling area. As usual, the colt had been on his best behavior.

However, now that he was in the walking ring, Star was beginning to get edgy. For the hundredth time Christina wished she could be riding her beloved colt. They had always managed to calm each other down before a race.

The jockeys began entering the walking ring. Melanie came over, looking very professional in her blue-and-white silks. "Hey, Star," she said, stroking the colt's face. "You ready to win this one for Christina?"

"If he breaks well, take him straight to the rail," Ashleigh told Melanie. "If possible, try to keep him behind Magic Trick and Celtic Mist, who should set a good early pace. But if he's running for you, don't hold him back too much."

Melanie nodded. "I think he's going to perk up once he sees these other horses, Chris. One look at Celtic Mist in front of him will be enough."

Christina looked across the walking ring, where Brad Townsend was giving last-minute instructions to Emilio Casados, Celtic Mist's jockey. Brad had stopped by Star's stall earlier, but he had barely said anything to either her or his son.

"Usually when my dad stops saying nasty things to

you, that means you've earned his grudging respect," Parker had said. "Did something happen while you were at Townsend Acres?"

Christina had shrugged, not ready to go into details about the deal she'd made with Brad.

But now, as she watched Brad give his jockey a leg up into the saddle, Christina realized that she had developed a grudging respect for the owner of Townsend Acres. While she didn't agree with Brad's need to display his wealth or with his aggressiveness in business, her time at Townsend Acres had helped her understand him better.

"You okay, Chris?" Melanie asked.

Christina quickly turned back to Star. "Yeah, I'm fine. I was just thinking that Mom's right. If Star kicks in, just let him run. Don't hold him back."

"I won't," Melanie replied. She placed her hands on the saddle in preparation for Mike's leg up. "I'll ride the best race that I can, Chris."

"I know you will," Christina said. She gave Melanie a thumbs-up while trying to swallow back the butterflies in her stomach. Watching was definitely worse than riding.

The escort rider approached them, ready to lead Star onto the track.

Christina held up her hand. "Wait. Please give me a second." She wheeled her chair to Star's head. The colt bent his neck, putting his head in her lap. "You know I love you no matter what happens, but you and I both also know that you can win. Try to forget about everything that's been going on lately. Just remember how much you love to run on the track, okay? Just run your hardest." Christina kissed Star's forehead and rubbed his ears. "Good luck, boy."

"What's taking so long?" Christina asked, twisting her program nervously in her hands. Dragon Prince, the horse with the fifth post position, was refusing to load. Having ridden several horses that disliked starting gates, Christina was usually sympathetic to the jockeys, but this day the wait seemed excruciating.

Parker reached over and took the program away from Christina. He put his hand over hers. "It's going to be okay," he whispered.

Christina squeezed Parker's hand and then leaned her head against her boyfriend's shoulder. Allie and Cindy were sitting beside them. Allie's face was chalk white. Both Parker and Cindy had offered to take her somewhere else, but she had insisted that she wanted to stay. Christina had wanted to comfort her, but she found it hard to talk around the nervous lump in her throat.

At last the track attendants pushed Dragon Prince into the gate, and the sixth and seventh horses quickly followed. Star, who would be breaking from the eighth post position, was next to load. As he walked in without protest, Christina focused on his stride, looking for a spring that would indicate he was ready to run. She didn't find anything.

Christina let go of Parker's hand as the final horses loaded, and she sat forward in her wheelchair, almost as if she were in the saddle. She thought about what she would be doing if she were in the starting gate. She would lean forward and whisper words of encouragement in Star's ear before settling into her crouch and grabbing a chunk of Star's copper mane.

Ring! The starting bell rang, and the gates slammed open. Twelve Thoroughbreds lunged from the gate.

It took Christina a moment to separate Star from the sea of surging horses. The colt had broken a bit sluggishly, and he was pushed wide as the horses rounded the first turn. Even from a distance, Christina could tell that Star's heart wasn't in the race. The colt's head was up, and he wasn't extending his stride.

"Come on, Star!" Christina yelled. "Run! I know you can do it!"

The horses spread out down the backstretch. Celtic Mist and Magic Trick had opened up a length lead on the rest of the field, but Gratis had a good position on the rail and was within easy striking distance. Star was tenth in the field, running alongside the late closers. Melanie had gotten the colt to lengthen his stride, but Star still acted like a horse who was just going through the motions. Christina had never known him to stay so far back willingly.

"Around the far turn, it's Magic Trick with a half-length lead over Celtic Mist. Dragon Prince remains in third over

Gratis. Further back, Storm Rider is starting to make his move, and Wonder's Star has moved up to sixth. And down the stretch they come!"

"Go, Star! It's now or never!" Christina shouted. "Run, boy, run!" She gripped the edges of her wheelchair so tightly that the metal left impressions in her palms. She knew that if Star didn't go into his superdrive soon, the race would be lost.

Storm Rider found his best stride first, shooting past Gratis and a quickly fading Dragon Prince. As Storm Rider flew by him, Gratis also seemed to gain renewed motivation. Aaron guided Gratis through a gap between Dragon Prince and Celtic Mist, and the colt drew even with the Townsend Acres colt. Yet despite strong challenges from Gratis and Storm Rider, the early leaders were not giving up without a fight. Celtic Mist and Magic Trick, who still clung to a slim lead, both dug in.

Christina waited for Star to join in this intense game of racehorse leapfrog. He never did.

Star managed to gallop past Dragon Prince in the final yards before the wire, but by then four other horses had already crossed the finish line.

"And Magic Trick goes wire to wire to win it!" the announcer cried. "Storm Rider is second, and Celtic Mist hangs on for third."

Christina felt warm tears pricking at the edges of her eyes, but she pushed them back resolutely. Now wasn't the time to cry. She was Star's owner, and she needed to get down to the track to make sure her colt was all right.

Everyone at Whitebrook was subdued as they went through the postrace motions. Ashleigh made some comment about how Star's long layoff had probably been a factor, but Christina could tell that her mother was only trying to make her feel better.

Strangely enough, Christina was probably the least surprised by the loss. She had known there was something wrong with the way Star was training, and unlike her parents and Melanie, she hadn't really expected a race-day miracle.

Christina kept up the facade that she was all right with this loss as her parents checked Star for injury and Parker and Joe sponged the colt down. She even managed to convince everyone she was okay and just needed time alone with Star.

Only once everyone had left did Christina allow herself to give in to her disappointment. She buried her face in Star's neck and cried.

8

As Allie rode Sterling Dream, a dark gray Thoroughbred mare, toward a four-foot rail, Christina felt as if she were watching the person she had been before Star had come into her life. Under Allie's steady guidance, Sterling soared over the jump, clearing it with several inches to spare. Allie praised the mare as she pointed the horse toward the next jump on the course, a three-and-a-half-foot parallel with a wide spread.

Three years before, Christina had been an avid three-day eventer. She and Parker had talked about competing in the Olympics together. Star had changed everything, focusing Christina's love for horses on racing instead of eventing. After much thought, Christina had sold Sterling to Samantha in order to focus on working with Star.

Not that I've done that very well, Christina thought glumly. In the four days since the Gold Cup, it had been hard for her to think positively. Even a return to Kentucky and a doctor's visit at which she'd been given a set of crutches hadn't cheered her up.

Christina's crutches were propped against an unused jump as she sat at the center of the arena and watched Allie jump the horse she once had planned to take to the Olympics. Although she was thrilled to have the extra mobility, Christina also had to admit that using crutches was harder than it looked. After just one day, her arms ached from supporting her weight.

"Great work, Allie!" Samantha called as Sterling landed perfectly after the oxer. "Now that I know what you can do, I'm going to have to convince that sister of mine to bring you here more often!" Samantha turned to Christina. "She concentrates so hard when she's going up to a jump that you just know she's going to make it over."

"She looks amazing on Sterling," Christina agreed. "I can't wait to see her on her own horse." Even though she was no longer jumping, Christina still enjoyed watching good eventing riders. Of course, her favorite horse and rider combination was Parker and Foxy. Thinking of her boyfriend, she added, "I bet Parker would love to give Allie some lessons."

"He probably would," Samantha said. "Isn't Parker's

meeting with the United States Equestrian Team representatives today?"

Christina nodded. "He said that he would call either you or me the second it's over."

"Since I taught him everything he knows, he'd better call me first," Samantha teased. She watched as Allie began walking Sterling on the rail to cool the mare out. "Do you think Allie would be interested in helping me teach?"

"Maybe," Christina replied. Five months pregnant with twins, Samantha was definitely starting to show, and her doctor had recently cautioned against too much strenuous activity. It would be good for her to have someone like Allie helping with the beginners. "I think Allie likes having something to do." She told Samantha about how Allie had helped get Star ready for the Gold Cup.

"I was like that after my mother died," Samantha said somberly. Samantha's mother had died in a riding accident when she was twelve. "It takes a while to get past that shocked and numb stage."

"Was there anything anyone could have done to help?"

"All we can do right now is listen when she wants to talk to us," Samantha replied. "She'll have to decide on her own to accept her new life, and I think she will. I can't see Cindy being anything but a great parent. But it's not going to happen right away." Samantha sighed, putting a hand on her rounded belly. "When my mom died, I thought nothing would feel like home ever again. Nothing did until we came to Kentucky." Samantha shook her head, as if clearing her thoughts, then called to the young girl, "Walk her around a couple more times, Allie, and then you can put her back in her stall."

"Is Kaitlin going to ride Sterling today?" Christina asked. Samantha was leasing the mare to Kaitlin Boyce, a high school senior. Kaitlin had come a long way with Sterling in the year and a half that they'd worked together.

"No, she's got some sort of community service event at school," Samantha replied. "I'm getting a little worried about her. She's been canceling lessons a lot lately, and she decided to skip a schooling show a couple of weekends ago. I think she's feeling peer pressure to do more typical teenage activities."

"That happens to everyone," Christina assured Samantha. Toward the end of her senior year Christina had felt some regret because she had spent so much time with Star, missing out on many activities and trips with her friends. "She'll figure out what she wants."

Samantha stood up. "I hope so." She handed Christina her crutches. "I think I'm going to try Allie on Irish Battleship. I want to see her ride a cross-country course."

Irish Battleship was the daughter of Finn McCoul, the horse that Samantha had worked with during the six years she'd spent in Ireland, and Miss Battleship, the first horse Samantha and her husband, Tor Nelson, had bought together. Although Tor had originally tried to train Irish Battleship as a steeplechaser, Samantha had convinced her husband that the mare would do better on the eventing circuit. So far it looked as though she was right. Before she had been forced to stop riding because of her pregnancy, Samantha had won two local three-day events on the mare.

Allie's dark brown eyes seemed to brighten when Samantha praised her riding and offered her a chance to ride another horse. She eagerly groomed and tacked up Irish Battleship and then listened intently as Samantha talked about the mare's quirks.

Cross-country had always been Christina's favorite part of three-day eventing. She had loved the thrill of galloping toward solid jumps, soaring over them, and then landing softly on the grass, ready to start the cycle all over again. In her opinion, the only better feeling in the world was galloping Star down the homestretch.

At that thought, Christina's mood darkened. How was she going to help Star? On the flight home Cindy had tried to cheer Christina up by telling her about Honor Bright, the dam of March to Honor. Because of a shoulder injury, Cindy had been forced to sit on the sidelines while Honor lost her maiden race. Cindy had been afraid that the horse's confidence had been shattered. But Cindy had come back and ridden Honor to victory in a stakes race only a month later. Christina knew that no matter how hard she pushed her recovery, there was no way she would be ready to race Star this year. It would be months before she even got her cast off.

But what if I found a way to ride Star with my cast on? Christina asked herself. Although the thought seemed far-fetched, she didn't dismiss it. After years of Samantha's training, Christina had learned to jump four-foot courses without her feet in the stirrups. If she could just get on Star's back again for a minute, maybe she would be able to figure out what was going on in his head and fix it. It was certainly something to think about.

"We're going to work over just two jumps today," Samantha was telling Allie. "We'll use the painted chicken coop over by the tree and the log pile right in front of me. I want you to really work on judging strides. When you were jumping Sterling, you sometimes took off a bit early. If you do that with Battle, she'll refuse."

Allie nodded, furrowing her brow in concentration. Despite her mood, Christina had to smile at Allie's expression. Christina knew she had always looked the same way when trying to correct one of her own bad habits.

Allie cued Irish Battleship into a steady canter and then into a ground-eating gallop. As the pair approached the chicken coop, three feet tall and four feet wide, Christina found herself reliving her eventing days, mentally going over everything Allie needed to do. *Count strides, squeeze with your legs, give with your hands, go with rhythm.* The instructions came back as though she'd heard them just the day before.

"You know, Chris, I could probably put both you and Allie to work here after the Breeders' Cup," Samantha said.

"Allie doesn't have the experience to give beginner lessons by herself, but you certainly do."

"What good is a riding instructor with a broken ankle?" Christina asked glumly.

Samantha put her arm around Christina. "We've all been injured, Chris. I know it's frustrating, but you'll only make yourself miserable if you don't find something else to do."

"I do have something to do!" Christina said. Realizing that she was almost shouting, she lowered her voice. "I have to find a way to make Star perform better in the Breeders' Cup."

"I know you do. But what about after that?"

Christina shrugged, realizing that she hadn't thought beyond the end of the month. She would be spending a few hours a week working on Dr. Reuter's research study, and she would have her classes, but then what?

"I think you could teach, especially with Allie's help," Samantha insisted. "She could help you set fences and walk alongside the problem students while you sat in the center and gave instructions."

Even if she wasn't sure whether Samantha was just giving her something to do out of pity, Christina did like the idea. And as Samantha's pregnancy advanced, her activity would probably be restricted more by her doctor. Perhaps Christina could be of some use. Christina looked over at Allie, who had been instructed to take the chicken coop again and build up more momentum before the jump.

Teaching a few lessons might give her a chance to help Cindy's foster daughter as well. "I'll do it," Christina replied at last. "But not until after the Breeders' Cup. Right now I have to focus on Star."

Allie reacted with much more excitement than Christina did when Samantha suggested that she might give some lessons. As Christina drove her back to Tall Oaks, it was all the girl could talk about.

Christina tried to keep up her end of the conversation, but she had to concentrate pretty hard on driving. Her doctor had fitted her with a slightly shorter cast the day before, and she appreciated the extra mobility.

Driving with a cast, however, proved to be more difficult than she had thought it would. The cast always seemed to be in the way, and it slowed her movement from the gas pedal to the brake. Because of this, Christina stuck to side streets, avoiding the larger, more congested roads.

"You and Sterling looked great together," Christina complimented Allie. "When I was watching, there was a second when I really missed eventing."

"What made you change your mind about eventing?"

"Mainly Star," Christina replied. "I wanted to work with him, and it didn't take long for me to realize that I couldn't be fair to both Star and Sterling." Christina paused as she negotiated a sharp turn. "There was also the parent factor. When I was young, my mom really wanted me to be interested in racing, and because she pushed me so hard, I rebelled. It took me a while to realize that I had ignored so many of the good things about racing because of my stubbornness."

"Mom and Dad were just the opposite of your parents," Allie said. "They realized I was fascinated with racing, and they tried to steer me toward other horse sports. When I was little, I used to crouch over my rocking horse, pretending I was winning the Kentucky Derby. But Mom and Dad told me they didn't want me spending too much time at the track yet, so they got me interested in jumping instead." Allie had turned away from Christina, pressing her face against the window as if she was looking for something far away. "After Mom died, Dad started bringing me to the track more. He even let me ride some of the escort ponies and put me on the calmer racehorses."

"You should talk to Cindy about that," Christina said. "My mom is always comparing Cindy to my cousin Melanie. Both of them wanted to be jockeys when they were even younger than you are. And they loved the fact that my mom let them work with the racehorses even though most trainers would have said they were too young."

"I don't know if that's what I want anymore," Allie whispered. "After seeing what happened to Dad, I—I just—I can't—" A choked sob escaped from Allie's throat. The girl buried her face in her hands. Her small shoulders were shaking.

Christina pulled over onto the side of the road, not sure what to say. Allie had been in the stands when her father died. There probably wasn't an hour that went by where she didn't see those images in her head. Christina unbuckled her seat belt and put an arm around Allie's shoulders. Allie didn't resist.

"If you want to talk about it, I'm here," Christina said softly. "I won't even pretend that I know how hard it is, but I want to help."

For several minutes Christina just held Allie against her, letting the younger girl cry. The sobs brought tears to Christina's own eyes. No matter how hard she thought things were for her just then, Allie had been through so much more. It was a wonder that the experiences hadn't made Allie angry or bitter.

"Is there anything I can do?" Christina asked as Allie's sobs began to slow.

Allie shook her head.

Christina turned the key in the ignition. "Why don't we go get some ice cream?" she suggested. When Allie didn't say anything, she started driving. Out of the corner of her eye, she saw Allie grab a box of tissues from the backseat.

Christina waited quietly while Allie composed herself. She wanted the younger girl to speak first.

"I'm sorry," Allie whispered at last. "It's just that every time I think about riding on the track—" Allie stopped, swallowed hard, and tried again. "I can't stop thinking

97

about how Dad died. Every night before I go to sleep, I think about how Firework and Dad went down, and how another horse landed right on top of them."

Just the thought of that accident was enough to make Christina feel sick. She remembered the brief clip she'd seen from the Matron Stakes. Her body had dangled limply, still attached to Charisma at the stirrup. She would have been helpless if another horse had fallen on top of her.

"I keep making these wishes," Allie continued, still sniffling. "When Mom died, I kept wishing that it hadn't happened, that I would wake up one day and she would still be here. But with Dad, one of the things I keep hoping for is that someone would tell me what I'm supposed to do now—how I'm supposed to go on."

"Do you think you'd like the answer even if someone gave it to you?"

Allie wiped her eyes with a tissue. "Probably not," she admitted. "I've never liked doing things other people tell me to do if they don't give me a good reason." She let out a laugh that almost sounded like a sob.

"There's no road map for what you're going through," Christina said. "You just have to trust yourself."

"But what if the only thing that makes me feel better is not to think about it?"

"Then maybe it means that this isn't something you can think about all at once. Maybe it's something you're going to have to come to terms with slowly." Christina turned right at a stoplight and then pulled into the parking lot of the shopping center. "In the meantime, you know you can always talk to me, right?"

Allie nodded. "Thanks for listening."

"Anytime." Christina turned off the car. "Now, let's go get some ice cream. My treat."

9

WHEN A RINGING NOISE WOKE CHRISTINA FROM A DEEP sleep, she instinctively reached for her alarm clock to hit the snooze button. The noise didn't stop.

Looking at the illuminated numbers, Christina realized that it was only 2:21. The noise was coming from her cell phone, which was on her desk. She was tempted to ignore the sound and go back to sleep, but the only person who could be calling was Parker. Christina had tried to call him several times before going to bed, but he had not answered. Groaning, she turned on a lamp and reached for her crutches.

Christina managed to hobble over to the phone just before her voice mail picked up. "Hello?" She sank down into her desk chair.

"Sorry to wake you, Chris, but I really need someone to talk to." Parker sounded oddly subdued.

"It's okay. I've been worried," Christina replied. Her mind was waking up now that she realized that Parker was upset. "What happened?"

"Mark Donnelly offered me another grant to cover my training expenses for the winter," Parker told her.

"That's great," Christina said. The captain of the United States Equestrian Team had taken an interest in Parker after the Rolex event in Kentucky, giving him the grant to train in England.

Parker continued as if he hadn't heard Christina. "But he also said that he's adding my name to the developing-rider list instead of to the winter training list."

"That's a start, isn't it?" Christina asked, trying to stay upbeat. The winter training list, which Parker had desperately wanted his name to be on, included the country's top riders. Many of them had competed in the Olympics. Training with riders on this list meant regular sessions with the team captain and the country's top trainers. "Many developing riders end up on the seasonal training lists."

Parker sighed. "I know. I just thought that after Burghley, Captain Donnelly would want me on the team."

"But you're definitely on their radar now," she pointed out. "If you keep doing well in the four-star events, they'll have to move you up."

"I've been up all night trying to convince myself of that," Parker said. "I didn't want to call you after I heard because I was so upset, and I needed time to sort things out in my head." Parker sighed again. "I know that when I talk to Sam, she'll just tell me I need to be patient. She'll say that I'm young and I'll get my chance eventually. But sometimes I get sick of waiting for eventually."

"You know you're talking to the wrong girl, right?" Christina joked. "I've never been patient about anything when it comes to Star. I guess I feel like I just don't have the time. I mean, he has only a few good years of racing before he's retired. You're lucky that eventing horses can compete longer."

"Yeah, I am," Parker conceded. "I don't mean to sound ungrateful, Chris. I know this is a great opportunity. It just wasn't quite what I wished for."

"But you're going to be there soon," Christina said. "And when you're standing on the podium to receive your gold medal, I fully expect to be acknowledged for all the help I gave you along the way, including these middle-of-the-night phone conversations."

Parker laughed. "You know I'll tell them how great you are. Anyway, I should probably let you get back to sleep. Is Star going to be working tomorrow?"

"No, we're waiting until Friday to put him back into heavy training. Not that the Gold Cup took too much out of him."

"Well, I'll be back tomorrow afternoon, and we can start thinking of ways to make your silly horse run again," Parker said. "Good night, Chris. I love you."

"I love you, too, Parker." Christina hung up the phone. When she crawled back into bed, she fell asleep with a smile on her face.

"Hello, my name is Christina Reese, and I have an appointment with Dr. Dietrich at noon." Christina slumped against her crutches as she waited for the receptionist to check the schedule on Friday. It had been a long morning, and she had barely made it to Willowglen Equine Clinic on time.

The morning had begun with Star's first exercise session on the track. While Melanie had only ridden the colt at a trot and a canter, Star had seemed listless and unresponsive. Both Ashleigh and Melanie had suggested that Star might still be tired after the race, but Christina knew better. Star had always been a bundle of energy when she worked him on the track after a week's layoff.

Because of Star's performance that morning, Christina was growing more determined to try her plan of getting on his back. In nine days she would finally be fitted with a shorter cast, one that would end just above her knee. There had to be some way she could ride Star then.

Melanie had also taken Jinx out on the track that morning. That had been a disaster. Jinx had bolted, spun around, and started galloping the wrong way on the track. Melanie was at a loss about how she was going to get Jinx ready for another race before the end of October.

After the workouts, Christina had gone to her biology

and chemistry classes. Although she had tried to keep up with schoolwork while she'd been in New York, Christina had fallen behind in her reading, and she was still trying to catch up.

A young woman wearing light blue scrubs walked into the reception area. "Are you Christina?" she asked. When Christina nodded, she said, "Hi, I'm Karrie. I'm also working on the suspensory ligament study. Angela—Dr. Dietrich—asked me to show you around."

"Hi, Karrie." Christina tried to balance on her crutches so that she could shake Karrie's hand.

"Don't worry about it, Christina. I was on crutches after knee surgery this summer, and I was never able to manage the handshake thing," Karrie said with a friendly smile. "Why don't you come on back?"

Karrie gave Christina an impromptu tour as they walked. Willowglen wasn't as big as Starting Line, but Christina appreciated the careful attention to detail. The examining areas and the operating and imaging rooms were all designed with the horses' comfort in mind.

"Usually, either Angela or Justin—that's Justin Browne, the other vet in the practice here—spends the morning doing surgeries, but Friday morning both of them schedule visits to their clients' farms so they can check on recuperating horses," Karrie told her. "Angela just called to say that she would be running late because of traffic on the freeway."

"Do you always call the vets by their first names?" Christina asked.

"Yeah, they like to keep things informal," Karrie replied. She opened the door of a small room next to one of the veterinarians' offices. The room had two desks that were covered with papers. There was a computer at each desk. Karrie gestured to the computer to their right. "This is where you're going to be working." Karrie pulled out a chair. "Sit down, and I'll show you some of the data."

For the next twenty minutes drug dosages, movement scores, and statistical parameters swam through Christina's mind. She tried to stay focused as Karrie explained each column on the spreadsheet. Owners in the study were supposed to record the amount of medication that they gave their horse each day. They were also asked to rate the horse's mobility on a 1-10 scale. Meanwhile, the vets had their own scale for judging the horse's movement as well as objective measures of improvement such as flexibility and gait tests.

"I know it sounds like a lot," Karrie said as she opened a new spreadsheet. "But it actually doesn't take too long to learn."

"Did I mention that math wasn't my best subject in high school?" Christina asked, rolling her eyes.

Karrie laughed. "I don't think it was the best subject for any of us, but I've come to appreciate statistics more. Now, why don't we go through this one together?"

They were halfway through the second spreadsheet when a knock at the door interrupted them. Christina looked up to see a woman wearing darker blue scrubs and a long white coat standing in the doorway. "Hey, Karrie. I take it you haven't managed to scare Christina away with all these statistics yet," the woman teased.

"I don't think jockeys scare easily," Karrie replied. "Christina, meet Dr. Angela Dietrich."

Angela walked over and shook Christina's hand. "Dr. Reuter tells me that you're thinking of becoming a vet."

"I'm considering it," Christina said. "I was hoping that getting some experience at a clinic would help me make a decision."

"Despite what you may have heard, it's not an easy life," Angela told her. "I'm on call every other night, which usually means that there are several nights each month when I have to come in to do an operation. And there are some times when I'm not sure that I'm even helping the horse. Sometimes an owner will tell me to do everything in my power to keep a horse alive, and I have to look into that horse's eyes, realize how much he or she is suffering, and still continue giving what I know will be futile treatments."

Christina looked away. She remembered what Dr. Reuter had told her after he operated on Callie. He had said that even if he did everything in his power, Callie would still live a horrible life, confined to a stall and unable to walk for more than a few minutes at a time. As hard as it had been to let Callie go, that had been the right decision.

"I know you've seen horses suffer at the racetrack, and since you're a jockey, I don't need to tell you how hard it can be to work in a male-dominated world," Angela continued. She softened her tone and added, "I'm not saying all of this to scare you. I just want you to come into this knowing the downsides. But there are so many positives, too. Today I visited a horse that had emergency surgery for a twisted intestine six weeks ago. He's going to make a full recovery." Angela looked over Christina's shoulder at the spreadsheet on the computer screen. "I also got a call from Dr. Reuter telling me that we got another grant for our suspensory ligament study, which means we can enroll another thirty horses and upgrade some equipment."

"Congratulations," Christina said, still trying to process the vet's words. They had intrigued her rather than scared her away. It would be interesting to learn the unique challenges of the veterinary world.

"Thanks," Angela replied. "Anyway, we've probably bored you long enough with data. Why don't you come make the rounds with me? I'll show you how to give some injections. You've probably given pain or medication shots to your own horses before, right?"

Christina nodded. She stood up and took her crutches from Karrie. "I learned to give a lot of different shots when my horse was sick last year."

"Yeah, I remember reading about Wonder's Star's mysterious illness," Angela said. "Well, let's see what you've learned."

• • •

"Forty-five and four-fifths seconds for the half mile!" Ashleigh called as Melanie finished her breeze. "We've got to get him looking sharper than this!"

In the past week Christina had heard so many poor breeze times that this additional one only left her numb. They had tried several things to make Star run. Two days earlier Ashleigh had even simulated a race, having Star and several other horses break from the practice gates and gallop for half a mile. Star had come in second, but he should have beaten all the other horses easily.

"I don't know what else we can do, Chris," Ashleigh said, rubbing her forehead wearily.

Christina traced a pattern in the dirt with her right crutch. She had been fitted with a shorter cast the day before. Although her doctor had told her that her ankle was healing, she also said it was a slow process and that Christina still needed to be very careful to avoid causing further injury. "If Star keeps running like this, do you think we should scratch him from the Classic?" she asked. While Christina wanted Star to run in the Classic, she knew that a poor performance there would do him more harm than good.

"We've still got another week before we ship him to Lone Star Park. Let's not think about that yet," Ashleigh replied.

Christina looked up at her mother in surprise. She had wanted her mother to dismiss the possibility of scratching

Star entirely. All week Ashleigh had been saying that they would find an answer. Now her mother seemed to have run out of ideas.

But Christina knew that the burden of coming up with a solution didn't fall on her mother. Since she knew Star best, it fell on her. And to figure out anything new, she was going to have to get on Star's back.

10

THE CONSTELLATIONS WERE STILL PLAINLY VISIBLE AGAINST
the night sky as Christina and Melanie entered the barn.
Christina moved quickly toward Star's stall.

"Are you sure about this?" Melanie asked, reaching for
Star's grooming equipment.

Christina nodded. "There are only two weeks left until
the Breeders' Cup, and this might be the only way I can get
through to Star. I have to try." She ran a currycomb along
Star's back. Most high-strung racehorses didn't stand still
while they were being groomed, but Christina trusted Star
not to move and make her lose her balance.

"What exactly are you hoping to do?" Melanie began
picking out Star's feet.

"I don't know. I've just always been able to think better

110

when I'm riding. I also think Star might focus more if he knew that I was still going to sit on his back every once in a while." Christina traded her currycomb for a soft brush. "It might not do any good, Mel, but I have to try something! You would do the same thing for Image or Jinx."

"The difference between Star's problem and Jinx's is that I know how to help Jinx," Melanie said, putting the saddle on Star's back. "Jinx doesn't like to be pushed. He's been pushed around and punished all his life because of his mean streak, and the only way he knows how to deal with that is by pushing back. The funny thing is that I don't want to push Jinx, either, but I have to so that I don't lose him."

"Maybe you could have Mom or Dad talk to Jazz. He respects their opinion." Christina fastened Star's girth, aware that they had to work quickly. They had less than an hour before the grooms would come into the barn and begin their morning chores.

"You mean he used to," Melanie replied as she bridled Star. "Now he doesn't see anything but the bottom line." Melanie fastened the bridle's noseband and chin strap. "All done. Where are you going to do this?"

"I was thinking we could just go up and down the drive. It's a pretty confined space, and we shouldn't disturb any of the other horses." Christina reached for her crutches. "I moved a stool out there yesterday so I could mount."

"Last chance to change your mind," Melanie said as she took Star's reins.

Christina shook her head. She was already making her way down the barn aisle.

The driveway outside the training barn had recently been a hive of activity as Ashleigh and Mike upgraded the farm's security system. Now that the construction was finished, there weren't any cars parked by the fences.

Christina shivered as she looked at the shadows under the floodlights. She was starting to wonder if this was a good idea. She had never ridden Star in the dark. What if she upset him?

But the consequences of doing nothing seemed worse. Christina hopped onto the stepstool, holding on to a wooden railing for balance. Her right leg was shaking.

"Are you ready?" Melanie asked softly. She was walking Star in slow circles. Christina could tell from Star's jerky gait that the colt was unnerved.

Christina clung to the railing for a moment longer, gathering her courage. Then, reminding herself that she had never been scared of riding Star before, she motioned for Melanie to lead the colt over to the stepstool.

Star tossed his head as Melanie stopped him in front of the stool. "It's okay, boy," Melanie soothed, tightening her grip on the reins.

Christina let go of the railing with one hand, reaching for Star's saddle. When her hand was firmly gripping the soft leather, she did the same thing with her left hand. She could feel Star's quivering muscles beneath her. "I'm going to vault on," Christina told Melanie shakily. "It's probably going to startle him, so I need you to make sure he doesn't move."

"Go ahead. I've got him."

Taking a deep breath, Christina pushed off with her right leg, transferring all her weight to her arms. She felt Star shift beneath her, but fortunately the colt did not spook. Quickly Christina put her right foot in the stirrup. Once she had shifted her weight over that stirrup, she moved her hands toward Star's neck and leaned forward. Grunting with effort and pain, she slid her left leg over Star's back.

"Are you all right?" Melanie asked.

For a moment Christina was in too much pain to reply. The movement had sent sharp spasms up her leg. At last she sat back in the saddle. Despite the pain, she felt as though this was where she belonged. "I'm okay," Christina told Melanie as she tried to shift her weight in a way that wouldn't stress her ankle. "I'm just having a little trouble with balance." Her heavy cast was pulling her to the left. "I can take the reins now."

"I think I'll hold on for a few minutes," Melanie said. "I want to make sure you're okay. You ready to walk?"

"Yeah, let's go." Christina gathered the reins in her hands. She pulled at them experimentally, but Melanie's hold was blocking her ability to signal directly to Star.

Star set off at a brisk walk. Each jarring step sent a spasm of pain through Christina's entire left leg. She gritted her teeth against it. "Attaboy, Star," she whispered.

"Can you believe it? It's just the two of us again." She patted Star's neck.

Star relaxed under her touch. The colt began walking quietly, stretching out his neck. Christina sat up straighter in the saddle, starting to enjoy the ride. Everything looked so much better on horseback.

"I'm going to let go now, but I'll be right beside you in case anything happens." Melanie released the reins, and Christina quickly gathered them. She was really riding again!

"Thanks, Mel," Christina said, unable to stop smiling. Now all she had to do was figure out how to make Star run.

A flash of headlights illuminated the driveway as a car drove past on a nearby road. Star lurched forward into a frantic trot, throwing Christina onto his neck.

"Whoa, Star, whoa!" Christina couldn't keep the panic out of her voice. She couldn't control Star when she was so off balance.

"Hang on, Chris. I'll grab the reins."

Christina wanted to protest, but Star's bouncing trot was making her cast slam against the colt's side. Her ankle hurt so much that her vision was blurring. "Please, Star. Please stop for me," she begged. "Please, boy." She slipped sideways in the saddle and knew she was about to fall. Frantically she tugged at the reins.

On the second tug, Christina felt a resistance that told her Melanie had taken hold of the reins. Melanie also put a hand on Christina's side, steadying her.

Blinking to get rid of the gray haze in her vision, Christina repositioned herself in the saddle. Although she managed to regain her balance, her body still slumped forward. "I think I should get off now," she heard herself saying. Her voice sounded far away, and there was a growing rush of blood in her ears. The only thing that was keeping her from passing out was the fiery throbbing in her ankle. Had she done something to injure it again?

Christina took deep breaths, trying to calm herself down. "We're okay, Star," she mumbled, repeating the words like a litany. "We're okay. We're okay."

Melanie led Christina to the stepstool. For a moment Christina wasn't sure if she would be able to get off, but luckily, the pain in her ankle abated, going from deep throbs to more bearable twinges. Christina put her right foot back in the stirrup, centered her weight there, and then carefully and slowly slid her left leg over. Once her leg was clear, she used her arms to support her weight as she lowered her right foot to the stool.

As Melanie led Star away from the stool, Christina limped to the ground. She sank down, not even able to summon the energy to stand. She looked over at Star. The colt was breathing hard, and despite Melanie's efforts to calm him down, he was still trying to prance from side to side.

Christina closed her eyes. It hurt her to see Star so agitated, especially since she was the one who had done this to him. She had tried so hard to help Star, but in the end she had done much more harm than good.

115

• • •

Thump. Thump. Thump.

"Are you sure this is a good idea?" Christina asked, resisting the urge to cover her ears to drown out the sound of Jinx's rhythmic kicking.

"Like you, I don't have a choice," Melanie replied. "Jinx isn't doing well at Whitebrook, so a change of scenery is my only hope."

"Well, I hope your idea works better than mine," Christina said glumly. Her ankle still ached from the morning's debacle, but she'd been forced to pretend that everything was okay while going to class and working at the vet clinic. Not surprisingly, she had not gotten much done in the way of learning biology or analyzing data.

Another consequence of her morning ride was that Star had turned in his worst workout yet. The colt's skittish behavior had puzzled Ashleigh, and Christina hadn't been able to tell her mother the truth.

To thank Melanie for her help, Christina was accompanying her to Tall Oaks. Melanie planned to keep Jinx in an empty paddock there and drive over in the mornings to work her colt on the Tall Oaks track. Melanie reasoned that Jinx might put more of his energy into adjusting to his new environment rather than misbehaving.

"Can you do me a favor and call Cindy to let her know we're coming?" Melanie asked. "I'm going to need some help unloading this monster."

116

Thump. Thump. Thump.

Christina dialed Cindy's number, wondering if the Tall Oaks trainer knew what she was getting herself into.

A few minutes later Melanie pulled the trailer into the long Tall Oaks drive. Cindy was waiting for them in front of the barn with Beckie, one of the grooms.

"Why don't we get Jinx out before he literally kicks down the door?" Cindy suggested.

Melanie smiled ruefully. "Luckily, I wrapped his legs pretty well before we left." She unlatched the back door. "Let me go in first. I don't want Jinx to hurt any of you."

As Melanie, Cindy, and Beckie tried to maneuver Jinx out of the trailer, Christina moved away, knowing she would only be in the way if she got closer. She wandered through the barns, finally heading to the training track, where a bay horse was being exercised.

As Christina got closer, she recognized the bay as Rush Street, one of Tall Oaks' three-year-olds, and the rider as Allie. She went over to the rail, where Ben was supervising the work. "How are you, Christina?" Ben asked.

"I'm all right," Christina replied. "It looks like Allie's doing a great job with Rush Street." Allie had the colt going in a smooth canter.

"She is," Ben agreed. "Cindy's been letting her ride some of our gentler horses on the track. I worry about her a little, but Cindy tells me that we should encourage her to ride if she wants to." Ben raised his voice and called across the track, "He looks good, Allie. Why don't we end things with a half-mile gallop?"

"Are you planning to take Rush Street down to Lone Star Park?" Christina asked as she watched Allie cue the colt into a gallop. The bay colt had missed qualifying for the Breeders' Cup races because of an injury.

"Probably not. I think I'll wait for the winter races at Gulfstream," Ben replied. "He has another good year of racing ahead of him, and there's no point in rushing things." Ben watched his horse for a moment. "Look at him go."

Rush Street's long strides and fluid gait impressed Christina, but Allie's method of handling the colt impressed her more. Allie's gentle but firm style reminded Christina of her own, especially when it came to Star.

Star. An idea popped into Christina's head, and only her ankle kept her from jumping for joy. "I'll be right back, Ben," she said, gathering her crutches and hurrying back to the barn.

Cindy and Melanie were getting Jinx settled in his paddock when Christina hurried up to them, moving as fast as her crutches would allow.

"Is something wrong, Chris?" Cindy asked.

Christina shook her head. She took a deep breath, waiting for her idea to organize itself into sentences. "Do you think that Allie would do well with Star? I just saw her on Rush Street, and I think she rides a lot like I do. And maybe putting someone who rides like I do on Star might help him calm down and focus on running again. Since I can't ride, I was hoping—"

"Slow down, Chris," Cindy interrupted. "I think I know what you're getting at, but are you sure this is a good idea? Putting a new rider on Star this close to the Classic might just upset him more."

"I won't do it during a morning workout. It'll be in the afternoon, maybe even this afternoon," Christina explained. "I know it's a long shot, but I want to see what happens. Maybe it'll work. And if not, I'm not really any further back than I was before. You understand what I mean, Mel, don't you?"

Melanie nodded. "I think it's worth a try, Cindy."

"Well, go ahead and ask Allie what she thinks," Cindy said. "If she's willing to ride Star, then you have my permission."

That was all Christina needed to hear. She dashed back to the track, ready to convince Allie to come back to Whitebrook.

11

"OKAY, STAR. I KNOW MY LAST IDEA FAILED, BUT I THINK THIS one's going to work," Christina said while she waited for Allie to get the colt's saddle. Allie had seemed somewhat confused by Christina's insistence that she come back to Whitebrook to ride Star, but the younger girl had agreed. Melanie and Cindy had both offered to help with the training session, but Christina had told them to work with Jinx instead.

Now that Christina was back at Whitebrook, though, she was starting to have her doubts. She had planned things so that she, Allie, and Star would have the track to themselves while Christina's parents and Ian McLean, the head trainer, were in town, because she didn't want the pressure of an audience. But what if something went wrong? She wouldn't be able to react quickly enough.

"We'll keep it slow," Christina resolved. "And I'll stop you if I think things aren't working."

"Is this everything you want?" Allie asked, balancing an armload of tack as she entered the stall.

"Yeah, it's perfect," Christina replied. "I know I pushed you pretty hard to come here, Allie. If you don't feel like riding, that's okay."

"No, I want to try," Allie said. "I think he would be fun to ride."

"He is." Christina patted Star's neck. "I have a few pointers before you get on."

"What are they?" Allie looked up from saddling Star to show she was listening.

"First, Star usually doesn't do anything wrong, and he hates it when his rider assumes he's going to do something bad. I think that was part of the initial problem between him and Mel. Melanie's used to riding horses with behavior problems, so she tries to anticipate when they're going to spook or buck." Christina picked up a comb and worked a tangle out of Star's mane as she continued. "Also, Star responds best if you cue with your hands and legs and then supplement that with your voice. Finally, you have to work to earn Star's cooperation. He will run for anyone, but he won't run well unless he really trusts you and feels that you're willing to work with him rather than just push him around." Christina finished untangling Star's mane and ran her hand through it. "I know that sounds silly, but it's the only way I can describe how Star and I finally got in sync on the track."

"Actually, Dad used to say the same thing about some of his mounts. He would compare riding to negotiating." Allie's voice was subdued, but she sounded reflective rather than sad. She tightened Star's girth and then walked over to the colt's head. "Are you ready to negotiate, boy? We want to make Christina proud, don't we?"

Once Allie had mounted Star and eased him onto the oval, Christina asked her to trot a warm-up lap. "We'll see how he responds and take it from there."

Star took a few skittish sidesteps as Allie cued him into a trot. It took the colt several moments to settle into the gait, but once he did, he reminded Christina a little of the Star of old. The colt was lifting his feet high with every stride, and his ears flicked back and forth, showing that he was listening to his rider.

Christina felt a bubble of hope rising in her. Maybe Allie would be able to help her solve Star's problems. "Go ahead and canter when you get to the backstretch!" Christina called as Allie and Star passed her. "If he feels okay at the top of the homestretch, ask him to gallop!"

Allie nodded, showing that she had heard, but quickly turned her attention back to Star.

Star transitioned effortlessly into a smooth, even canter.

Christina could tell that the colt was eager to run. He was extending his head with every stride. Christina couldn't wait to see him at the gallop.

As Allie and Star rounded the far turn, Allie crouched deeper in the saddle and gave Star his head.

"Come on, Star!" Christina called. She could see the colt hesitating, and her heart sank. "Knead your hands along his neck!" she instructed. "Talk to him! Make him want to run for you!" Christina could tell Allie was frustrated. The young girl was moving in the saddle, trying to get the colt to listen. "Don't get after him so much with your legs and seat! Use your voice!"

Star cantered unevenly down the homestretch, never showing any signs of improvement. Christina kept calling out instructions, but she could see they were having little effect. "Pull him up!" she said when Star and Allie passed her. She had already come up with one plan that had hurt Star today. She didn't want this to be another one.

At Allie's signal, Star obediently dropped down to a slow trot and then a walk. Christina wished she could go back to the time Star would fight restraint, wanting to keep running.

"Thanks, Allie," Christina said as the girl rode Star back. She tried to keep the disappointment from her voice. "Maybe there isn't any way to get him back to his old form before the Classic."

"I don't know about that," Allie argued. Christina

looked up at her, surprised. "I think I could have gotten through to Star," Allie continued. "I just couldn't do it the way you wanted me to."

"What do you mean?"

Allie turned away from Christina's piercing gaze. "I'm just not sure that your instructions were—were helpful," she stammered. "I know you want to do the best you can for Star, but maybe there are other ways to ride him."

Protest surged within Christina, but she stayed silent, wanting to hear what Allie had to say.

"I can't ride Star the way you do. I don't think anyone can. But maybe if I work with him on my own, I can get through to him."

Christina leaned back against the rail, considering. She had been so sure that she knew the only way to get through to Star. After all, it had taken her two years of riding him to have the perfect moment that they'd shared at the end of the Belmont Stakes. She had wanted to save Melanie the effort of all that trial and error.

But she and Melanie had never ridden the same way. Melanie relied more on daring and aggressiveness and often pushed horses harder. Christina hadn't wanted Melanie to ride Star aggressively. Now she no longer knew if that was such a bad thing. By telling Melanie exactly how to ride Star, she had essentially taken away her cousin's greatest strengths, the things she had always admired about Mel's riding.

And what about Allie? Just because they had similar

riding styles didn't mean that Allie would react the same way she did in each situation. Star had been responding to Allie, and Christina had gotten in the way of that with all her criticism.

"I'm sorry, Christina. I shouldn't be telling you how to train your horse." Allie got ready to dismount.

"No, stay on," Christina said quickly, gathering her thoughts. "I want you to try it again. This time, do what you think you need to do to make Star run. Just listen to him. He'll tell you if he doesn't like something."

"Are you sure?" Allie still didn't settle into her jockey's crouch.

"Yes. I'd be really happy if you would give me and Star another chance," Christina replied. "Just canter him to the backstretch and then let him loose when you're ready." Christina ran her hand in circles around Star's neck, still trying to absorb all these realizations. "Be a good boy for Allie, okay?"

"We'll do the best we can," Allie said. Her dark eyes darted with nervousness.

"Relax," Christina told her, trying to smile. "Even if you don't make him run his best, you've still done as well as anyone else who's ridden him lately."

"He can do better," Allie insisted. She turned Star up the track and asked him to canter.

Christina gripped the railing tightly, watching them go. Was Star going to be too tired? Had her bad training techniques already sabotaged his chances of victory?

Christina's negative thoughts only multiplied as Allie rode Star down the backstretch. It was clear that the colt was fighting Allie as she asked for a gallop. Star was tossing his head, and his strides were short and choppy.

"Please, Star. I know I've been confusing you lately, but I know you're still the same horse that won the Belmont," Christina murmured, watching as Star gave a small buck.

Star bucked twice more. Christina wanted to help Allie get the colt under control, but she bit her tongue. Allie was keeping her seat, and the girl was engaged in her own negotiations with Star. Christina couldn't do anything to help.

Star switched leads as Allie guided him around the far turn. The colt tossed his head once more before stretching his neck forward.

"Attaboy!" Christina shouted. "Run, baby, run!"

Star rounded the turn and streaked into the homestretch. His long legs ate up the track as he lengthened his gait. For a second Christina almost felt as though she were on Star's back. She could practically hear the wind whipping through his mane and feel his powerful strides beneath her. "That's my Star," Christina whispered. "That's my Star."

Allie leaned down and said something to the colt. Star responded, quickening his pace. *Superdrive.* Star had reached his best gear.

Once they passed Christina, Allie stood in the stirrups, pulling Star back. The colt tried to stretch his neck forward to avoid the restraint.

126

Christina punched the air with her fist, as if Star had just won a race. In some ways this was an even bigger victory.

Usually the first place Christina went in the mornings was Star's stall. This morning she bypassed the barn, instead heading to the track. She had not discussed Allie's ride with anyone the night before. She didn't want to get everyone's hopes up until Star demonstrated improvement.

Ashleigh was already standing at the rail, watching as Dani Martens, one of the farm's exercise riders, breezed Ending Shadows. The two-year-old colt was maturing nicely, although he didn't have the speed that his stablemate March to Honor did.

"Good morning, Mom," Christina said. She stood by her mother's side, trying to figure out how to bring up her plan for Star.

"Good morning, Chris. What are you up to now?"

Christina smiled. Her mother could always guess when she had a new idea. "Today I'm going to tell Melanie to ride Star the way she rides Jinx."

"What?" Ashleigh looked away from the track in surprise.

"I've decided that I've spent too much time telling Melanie what to do. Maybe I should just let Mel ride the way she always does." Christina told her mother about Allie's ride on Star.

"You should have waited until someone else was

around," Ashleigh said, a note of concern in her voice. "What if Star had thrown Allie?"

"I had to act on what I thought," Christina insisted. "And I know Star. I would have stopped the workout if I thought he was going to do anything to hurt her."

Ashleigh looked away. "I grew up idolizing Jilly," she said in a strained voice. "She was everything I wanted to be. I used to think that when I became a jockey, we would move around the tracks together, like you and Melanie do. But then she married Craig and moved to the West Coast, and I got busy with things at Whitebrook. I feel like I owe it to Jilly to watch over her daughter now."

"I'm sorry, Mom," Christina apologized. Her mother's words left her subdued. Sometimes when she was around Allie, it was easy to forget what the girl had been through. "But I really did have things under control."

Ashleigh nodded. "I know you wouldn't jeopardize safety," she said. She turned back to the track, but Christina could still see the tension in her smile. "We'll try your plan today and see how it goes."

Christina spent the next hour by the rail, watching as the horses were worked in sequence. Star was last in Melanie's morning rotation.

"Any advice?" Melanie asked as she prepared to get on Star.

"I want you to close your eyes," Christina said. When Melanie looked at her as if she were crazy, Christina repeated the instruction. "Close your eyes. Now pretend

128

that Star is Jinx or any other horse you're familiar with. I want you to ride Star the way you would ride that horse. Forget everything else I've told you."

"I'm much rougher with Jinx than I am with Star," Melanie protested. "I don't want to lose Star's trust."

"You can't lose his trust when I never gave you a way to gain it," Christina pointed out. "I assumed that if you rode just like I did, then Star would accept you. Allie showed me I was wrong."

"You still haven't told me what happened with Allie."

"I'll tell you after the workout," Christina said. She didn't want Melanie to be upset if Star didn't respond as well as he had with Allie.

There were subtle changes in the way Melanie warmed Star up. She used her hands more than usual and changed Star's position on the track. Sometimes she would ride along the rail. Other times she would move to the middle. Christina knew her cousin often did this with Jinx to keep the colt interested.

Star seemed to be interested, too. His ears were moving back each time Melanie spoke, and he was cantering without hesitation.

"Let's see what happens at the gallop," Ashleigh decided. She signaled to Melanie.

At first Christina wondered if Melanie had seen the signal. Then she realized that her cousin had—she just couldn't get Star to listen. The colt's ears were pricked forward, and he had his head straight up in the air, like a horse in a parade.

Although she had ideas, Christina resisted the urge to say anything to Melanie. She had originally wanted her cousin to avoid the fights she'd had with Star in order to gain his trust. But what if those fights had been integral to their relationship? Melanie had ridden difficult horses before. Christina told herself that her cousin would find a way to work with Star.

By the time Star rounded the far turn, Melanie had him going in an uneven gallop. Christina waited for Star to come down the homestretch. She figured that Star would respond with a burst of speed, just as he had for Allie.

Nothing changed. Star continued tossing his head and fighting Melanie. But as they approached, Christina noticed that the colt was lowering his head.

"Let them go on," Christina told her mother.

"I don't want to tire Star out."

"He's not tired, and he's starting to listen. We need to end on a good note. Just give me another half mile," Christina argued. If she could have, she would have jumped up and down in frustration.

"Go another three-eighths of a mile!" Ashleigh called to Melanie. "I don't want to burn him out," she said to her daughter.

"Come on, Star! I know you can do this!" Christina yelled as Star and Melanie galloped past her. "I made a mistake before, but I'm trying to fix it now. Please let me!"

Star made his way through the next eighth of a mile without improvement. As they rounded the next turn,

Christina saw Melanie move the colt toward the rail. Star was so close that he was almost brushing up against it.

"Pretend like you're in a race, Star," Christina muttered under her breath. "There's an opening on the rail and you're going to shoot through it. The crowd is going wild, and there are horses all around you. You don't care about any of them. You know that you're going to run your fastest."

"Look, Chris!" Ashleigh cried.

Christina looked up just in time to see Star switch leads and lunge forward.

"That's it! Go!" Christina and Ashleigh were both cheering at once.

As if he could hear them, Star lowered his head and dug in, streaking into the backstretch. Melanie pulled up the colt as they passed the three-eighths pole. As he had the day before, Star fought the restraint.

Ashleigh put her arms around her daughter. "Good job, sweetie," she praised.

Christina shook her head. "Allie, Melanie, and Star did all the work. All I had to do was let them."

"I'm so happy for you, Chris," Parker said as they sat down at a local restaurant for dinner that night. "I knew you would find a way to get Star back on track."

"I hope I did," Christina replied. Star's workout seemed so far away now. She'd had a biology test that morning, and then she'd put in a long afternoon at the vet clinic. Dr. Reuter had sent a new batch of data for analysis, and just when she finished the preliminary work, Justin had invited her to watch a bone chip surgery. "We've still got a couple of works before we leave for Lone Star Park, so we'll see if it made any real difference."

"Of course it made a difference."

Christina shrugged. She took a sip of her soda and then sank back in her chair. She knew the day's events should have made her happy. So why wasn't she feeling that way?

Parker scooted his chair closer to Christina and then put an arm around her. "What's wrong, Chris?"

Christina stared at the flickering candle on the dinner table. "Star's three-year-old season will be over in two weeks, and I feel like I've made so many mistakes this year."

"What kinds of mistakes?"

"First I tried to rush him back after he recovered from his illness. Then I tried to change his running style before the Santa Anita Derby. The Kentucky Derby was a disaster, and because I couldn't stop thinking about that race, I think it affected my performance in the Preakness. And then there's the fact that I let Jessie upset Star before the Travers." Christina ticked off her mistakes on her fingers. "That's five big mistakes, not counting the ones I've made since I got injured, and what do I have to balance that? Just two perfect moments on the track: one in the Louisiana Derby and another in the Belmont."

"You can't look at it by the numbers," Parker protested.

"And you can't put a value on any of the things you named. What would you have traded that moment during the Belmont for?"

"I don't know," Christina admitted. "But I keep thinking that maybe I won't make it back all the way from my injury, at least not while Star's still racing."

"You don't know that."

Christina leaned against Parker's shoulder and closed her eyes. "When I was in the hospital, I told myself that I would find a way to heal faster than anyone expected. It was the only thing that kept me from crying myself to sleep in that first week. Now I've seen the X-rays. I can't ignore the evidence that I'm not going to be ready to ride for a while." Christina pulled away from Parker, trying not to let herself melt into an emotional mess in his arms. "I'm whining, aren't I?"

"A little," Parker answered. "But you're allowed to whine. If I were in your place, I'd try anything I could to get on Foxy's back."

Christina smiled sheepishly and told Parker about her ill-advised attempt to ride Star the day before.

"That sounds like the Christina I know," Parker said, chuckling. "I'm just glad you didn't get hurt."

"So am I." Christina took another sip of her soda, temporarily suppressing her doubts about her recovery. This wasn't something she'd be able to find an answer tonight. "So when is your first developing-rider training session?"

"The end of January. I'm going to have to make a pretty

big decision about that soon, though," Parker answered.

"What kind of decision?"

"The committee will let me list only two horses. Foxy will be my main horse, of course, but I don't know who to put down as my backup. Black Hawke's the logical choice, since he's more solid, but I have a feeling that Ozzie could be the better horse with more training. If I leave Ozzie behind, then he won't ever be consistent."

"Could someone else at the barn work either horse for you?" Christina asked.

"Well, I've thought about getting Allie to help with the show jumping, but it would have to be with Black Hawke, since Ozzie's so weird about everything," Parker replied.

"I'll be working at Whisperwood with Allie after the Breeders' Cup. Maybe I could help her with your horses," Christina suggested. "It's been a long time since I jumped competitively, but I think I still remember enough to teach the basics."

"I'm glad you and Allie are going to work at Whisperwood."

Christina nodded. "So am I. After the Breeders' Cup, I'll need things to keep me busy." Deep down, Christina wondered what she would do during the winter. How was she going to occupy herself when she couldn't do anything involved with racing?

12

A WEEK AND A HALF LATER CHRISTINA WAITED NERVOUSLY
in the doctor's office. She tried to look over her biology lab
report, which was due in two hours, but found herself
unable to concentrate. Why was the doctor taking so long
with her X-rays?

Christina leaned against the wall. Everyone at Whitebrook had left for Lone Star Park two days before. On Saturday Star had turned in his best workout yet for Melanie.
His time for the half mile was still a second slower than his
personal best, but Christina had a feeling that with a few
more works Star would be performing close to his peak.

Christina's flight to Dallas was leaving that evening.
She would be traveling with Cindy and Allie. Cindy had
delayed her flight because of paperwork problems in

enrolling Allie in high school. Cindy had been home-schooling Allie for the past few weeks to give her a chance to adjust to her new environment before starting at a new school, but Allie would start attending classes when they returned from the Breeders' Cup.

There was a knock at the door. Christina sat up, her heart racing. "Come in," she called shakily. She sat on her hands so that the doctor wouldn't notice they were trembling.

Dr. Liza Sher was one of the best sports medicine physicians in the state, and she specialized in ankle and leg injuries. During her first appointments, Christina had come to like the doctor because of her sense of humor and willingness to listen.

"Don't worry, Christina," Dr. Sher said when she saw Christina's expression. "I have some good news, even if you might not be too impressed."

"What do the films look like?" Christina asked. There was still a tremor in her voice.

Dr. Sher put the X-rays on the viewer. "I was checking the position of the plates and screws," she said. She pointed to the bright spots on the X-rays. The plates really stood out against the lighter bone. "The pins and plate in your fibula are going to have to be removed in two months, but we'll probably leave the pins in your ankle unless they bother you later."

"Does it look like the breaks are healing?"

Dr. Sher nodded. "You're very lucky."

Christina sighed with relief.

"Still, it's going to be a while before you're back on a horse again," Dr. Sher continued. "I have every reason to believe that you will regain full strength in your ankle, but I don't think it will happen before your horse starts racing next year."

"So when will I be able to ride again?" Christina asked, hoping she didn't sound too impatient.

"I don't know. You'll be able to start rehab once we take this cast off and do surgery on your fibula, but what happens then depends on what kind of pain you can take."

"I'll do whatever I can to be Star's jockey next year," Christina insisted.

"I know you will," Dr. Sher said gently. She looked at Christina and then back at the X-rays. "Off the record, I think you might be riding by late April, but on the record, I can't give you a reliable estimate." She winked.

Christina smiled. "Thanks, Dr. Sher." Now she had a date—something to aim for, something to try to beat.

Christina's good mood carried her through her biology class, keeping her alert during the lecture on protein synthesis. Even a disappointing grade on her biology test couldn't bring her down. She knew she hadn't studied well for that test because Star had been a distraction. She would be able to make it up next time.

"Are you ready to go to Texas?" Christina's lab partner,

Courtney, asked as Christina sat down next to her before chemistry.

"Definitely," Christina replied. "I can't wait to see Star again."

"But I'll bet that the joy of watching horses at the racetrack can't compare to learning about oxidation-reduction reactions," Courtney joked.

Christina laughed. "You've got me there. What are your plans for the week?"

Courtney shrugged. "The usual. A bunch of us were thinking about checking out the new club in Lexington. You should come out with us sometime—if you're not too busy traveling to racetracks, that is."

"I'll have more time after the Breeders' Cup," Christina said. "We should go out once I get back."

"Let's go ahead and get started," the professor began. He dimmed the lecture hall lights and projected his first slide onto the screen. Instead of his usual summary of learning objectives, it was a picture of a racehorse crossing the finish line. Christina immediately recognized the horse as Star. It was a picture of the two of them crossing the finish line at the Belmont Stakes. "First, I want to wish Christina and Star good luck in the Breeders' Cup. We'll be cheering for you, Christina."

The entire class clapped, and people in the front rows turned around to look at her. Christina could feel her cheeks reddening with embarrassment, but at the same time she was touched that people outside the racing community recognized how important this race was for her and Star. She promised herself that she would get to know her professors and her classmates better once she got back.

The chaos at Willowglen when Christina arrived after her chemistry class reminded her of the activity before a big race. Two horses had come in at once. One needed several dozen stitches to close a cut it had received during a fight with another horse. The other had some mysterious neurological illness.

Angela called Christina into the quarantine stall to help with the examination of the sick horse. It didn't take Christina long to realize the seriousness of the situation. The mare, a black quarter horse named Touchstone, was having trouble standing, and her legs wobbled each time she attempted to move.

"I don't understand," the owner was saying. "She's been a little lethargic for a few days, but we had a big show last week, so I thought that she was just bouncing back slowly. But when I went to check on her this morning, she was down in her stall."

Those words brought Christina back to the events of the year before, when Star had come down with a mysterious virus. It had started as simple lethargy after a race but soon developed into a systemic illness that had threatened Star's life. Star's neurological symptoms had been similar to these. Could that disease have come back?

"Have you taken Touchstone to any out-of-state events lately, ma'am?" Christina asked.

"Yes, the show was in Florida," the woman replied.

Fire 'n' Ice, the racehorse who had infected Star with the mysterious virus, had been training in Florida. "Can I talk to you for a second, Angela?" Christina asked. She didn't want to alarm the mare's owner until she got the vet's opinion.

Angela looked at her quizzically but nodded and followed Christina out of the stall. "What is it?" she asked once they were out of earshot.

"I think Touchstone might have the same virus Star had last year," Christina replied. She quickly explained Star's symptoms as well as the Florida connection.

"This could just be a coincidence," Angela said, looking skeptical.

"But what if that virus was spread by a certain insect or something like that?" Christina insisted. "It's possible that the insects would be localized to Florida in the fall." Christina's voice rose as she remembered how ill Star had been. She took deep breaths, reminding herself that Star was healthy now and that they had no evidence that this mare had the same disease. "Maybe you should call the place where the show was held and see if there are other sick horses."

Angela nodded. "That's not a bad idea," she agreed. "If it is the same virus, what treatment options are there?"

Christina shook her head. "The blood work never

showed anything. All Dr. Stevens could do was give Star fluids and use steroids to suppress his immune response."

"Well, we don't have the blood work results yet, but I suppose it wouldn't hurt to give the mare fluids. Would you grab a couple of liters of saline from the surgery suite?"

"Sure." Christina moved over to the sink, washing her hands carefully. She didn't want to transmit any diseases to the other horses in the clinic. As the warm water trickled through her fingers, Christina glanced back at the sick mare. She had been wrong about one thing when she had come up with only one highlight of the past year for Star. The greatest highlight of all had been his recovery from a disease that could have killed him.

"Ladies and gentlemen, due to thunderstorms in the Southeast, we are going to delay boarding for our flight to Dallas-Fort Worth International Airport this evening. The new boarding time will be eight-fifteen. Thank you for your patience."

Christina, Cindy, and Allie groaned in unison. They had been hovering by the glass doors, waiting for boarding to start.

"Well, we might as well make ourselves comfortable," Cindy said. "I'm going to grab some frozen yogurt. Do you two want to come?"

Christina was about to follow when she felt her cell phone vibrating in her backpack. Willowglen's number came up on the screen. "Do you mind getting me a small cup of strawberry?" she asked. "I want to hear how this horse is doing." Christina had spent her entire afternoon at the vet clinic helping Angela with the mare. None of the test results had come back before she left, but Angela had reached the show grounds in Florida and learned that two other horses from the show were sick.

"No problem," Cindy replied as Christina answered the phone.

"Hi, Christina. It's Karrie."

"Any news on Touchstone yet?"

"Angela thinks you might be right about the virus," Karrie said. "The blood work just came back negative. She wants to know the names of all the people who treated Star so that she can contact them for information."

"Well, the main vet was Dr. Stevens. He used to work at Townsend Acres, but now he has a clinic in Louisville," Christina said. She sat down in one of the blue plastic chairs in the waiting area, wishing that she hadn't been right in her diagnosis. "I think he'll know the names of the vets who worked with the horses down in Florida. You might want to check with Dr. Reuter, too. He knows all the Belmont vets and might be able to contact the people who worked with Fire 'n' Ice." Christina sighed. "How is the mare doing?"

"Not too good," Karrie admitted. "Angela's got her on fluids and painkillers, but she's thinking of trying a round of steroid therapy tomorrow." Karrie paused. "Hold on a

142

sec, Chris." Christina heard muffled voices on the other end of the line. She wondered if one of them was Angela's. If so, did the vet have any additional information? "Angela wants to talk to you," Karrie said after a pause. "I'll call you once we have more news."

"Thanks, Karrie." Christina heard rustling as Karrie handed the phone to Angela.

"Hi, Christina. I'm glad we caught you before your flight left," Angela said.

"So am I," Christina replied. "I don't know how much more useful information I can give you, though."

"Actually, I wanted to talk about your job here."

"Did I do something wrong?" Christina asked. She thought back to her last session at the computer. She had been working quickly to process as much data as she could before she left for the Breeders' Cup. Had she made a mistake?

The vet laughed. "It's nothing bad, Christina. I just wondered whether you would be interested in a part-time vet tech position in addition to your data analysis responsibilities. I know you're committed to other things, so you could work as much or as little as you want. I was thinking maybe two or three times a week, four hours per shift."

"That would be great," Christina said. Before her injury, she would have hesitated, not knowing how to balance racing and her other interests. For better or worse, that wasn't an issue at the moment.

"Fantastic! We'll discuss the details when you're back in town. Now I need to get back to Touchstone. Have a good flight."

"Thanks, Angela," Christina said. "Good luck with Touchstone."

"Good luck to you, too."

Christina hung up the phone. She checked her watch, remembering the last time she had been at the airport waiting to fly to a racetrack. Had it been only five weeks before? She'd thought there were so many possibilities for her and Star then.

Christina shook her head. She couldn't wallow in self-pity. There were still possibilities for her and Star now. Star would be running in the Classic in just four days, and she had plans for the winter. A smile played at the corners of Christina's mouth. Despite all that had happened in the past weeks, she still did have a lot to look forward to.

The Lone Star Park track was already filled with predawn activity when Christina made her way to the rail the next morning. At the gap she saw Melanie and Jinx. To her surprise, Aaron Evans was mounting the chestnut colt.

"Hey, Aaron," Christina said. She refrained from asking him why he was riding. "How are you?"

"I'm all right," Aaron replied. "I've been meaning to call you," he added. He looked her over with his intense brown eyes. His gaze stopped at her cast. "I'm sorry about your accident."

Christina shrugged. "It's okay. Are you here with Dreamflight?"

"Sort of. Patrick and Amanda have only one horse running, in the Distaff. Matter of Time reinjured his tendon a couple of weeks ago, and . . . well, Callie was their best horse other than Matt." Aaron paused. Christina could tell he was remembering Callie. So was she. "The Johnstons are using another jockey in the Distaff, but Cindy asked me to come down and ride Gratis in the Classic. And yesterday Melanie offered me a mount on her horse, who makes all the troublemakers from Dreamflight look like angels." Aaron stopped and waved toward the stands. Christina turned around and saw Jessica, a groom from Dreamflight. "Jess is really excited about my ride in the Classic," Aaron said. "She thinks we should head out to the East Coast next year. She'll groom and exercise-ride, and I'll try to get mounts."

Christina smiled. Back in June she had guessed that Aaron and Jessica would get together. "Well, if you're ever in Kentucky, you'll always have a place to stay."

"Thanks," Aaron said. He gathered Jinx's reins just as the colt took a small bunny hop backward. "I'd better get going." He turned the horse up the track. "We should get together for dinner sometime this week."

"Sure," Christina said. She moved out of the way so

that Aaron and Jinx had a clear path to the rail. Once Jinx had trotted away, Christina turned to her cousin. "Why did you ask Aaron to ride Jinx for you? Is something wrong?"

"Actually, I got the idea from you," Melanie replied. "During the plane flight up here, I was thinking about what you did for Star. Star doesn't run the same way for you as he does for me, but in the end, I can be almost as effective."

"What does that have to do with Jinx?" Christina asked.

"Well, I've been assuming that I was the best person to ride Jinx—"

"Of course you are! You were the one who got him to run in the first place."

"Let me finish," Melanie said. "I always assumed I was the best jockey for Jinx, but Star's turnaround in the last few days made me wonder how Jinx would do with someone who rides the way you do. I thought about trying Allie, but I was afraid Jinx would hurt her. So I asked Aaron, and it's paid off. Jinx responds to him better than he does to me."

"But you deserve to ride Jinx in the race tomorrow. You've done all the hard work." Christina couldn't believe that her cousin would just hand over control of her horse to someone else. "Besides, there's been so many moments at Whitebrook when you two have looked amazing together."

"This isn't a permanent thing," Melanie replied. She gave Aaron a thumbs-up as he and Jinx passed them at a canter. "Besides, it's normal for trainers to try new jockeys. We're just lucky at Whitebrook because we usually don't have to."

Christina remembered having that same thought a month earlier, when she'd visited Dr. Reuter's clinic and seen the two Whirlaway descendants. Perhaps what worked for Whirlaway would work for Jinx, and a jockey with a calmer presence would turn the horse around.

"I just need to jump-start Jinx for tomorrow's race," Melanie continued. "If he does well there, then I can think about the future. But if the race goes the way it did last time . . ." Melanie turned back to the track without finishing the thought.

Christina knew the decision to change jockeys must have been difficult for Melanie. She watched as Aaron cued Jinx into a gallop. The colt was all business. "They're going to do great tomorrow," she said confidently. "You're not going to lose Jinx."

13

EVEN THOUGH THE CROWDS FOR THE LONE STAR PARK
Juvenile were small compared to what the track was expect-
ing for the Breeders' Cup two days later, there were still a
sizable number of people crowded around the walking ring.
From her place in the stands, Christina could barely see
Melanie, Mike, and Jazz. Jazz had arrived that morning.
Christina didn't think that he and Melanie had exchanged
more than a few sentences in the hours before the race.

Aaron entered the walking ring wearing Jazz's trademark
emerald green silks patterned with white music notes.
Christina wondered what Melanie was telling him. Was her
cousin having second thoughts about not riding Jinx herself?

Christina looked down at her lap. What had once been a
program of the day's races was now a wad of crumpled

paper in her hand. But she wasn't the only nervous one in the group. Her mother was sitting at the very edge of her seat, gripping the chair so tightly that her knuckles were white. Apparently Ashleigh also knew that more than the race was at stake.

Melanie joined them in the stands moments before the start. Christina patted her cousin's shoulder, knowing Melanie didn't want to talk.

The bells rang, and the eight two-year-old colts leaped from the gate. Christina held her breath as the jockeys angled their horses toward the rail. She winced as she saw two horses bump into each other on Jinx's left, but Aaron was able to avoid them as he positioned Jinx just off the rail, a length behind the leaders.

"Sound Barrier takes an early lead with Surefire right behind him. On the rail, it's Hi Jinx and Great Beyond. . . ."

After the initial announcement of where the horses were, Christina ignored the announcer. She focused on Jinx instead. The distance between the first and last horses grew steadily shorter during the first half mile. Jinx continued to hold on to third.

"Go, Jinx!" Christina called as the wall of horses thundered around the far turn. Several were dropping back, but four horses, including Jinx, were still pursuing Sound Barrier, who still held a half-length lead.

"Come on, Jinx! Win this for us!" Melanie screamed. She was crouched forward in the seat, almost as though she were riding the race herself.

149

As if he could hear Melanie, Jinx changed gears, charging past Sound Barrier. But another horse, a late closer named Sail Away, flew by on the outside. Sail Away pulled a quarter length ahead before Jinx responded to the challenge.

Jinx and Sail Away matched strides as they approached the finish line. Jinx managed to cut Sail Away's advantage to a head, but the other colt maintained that advantage as the horses went under the wire.

"Sail Away wins by a nose!" the announcer cried as the horses crossed the finish line. "Then it's Hi Jinx in a very close second, with Sound Barrier a length behind."

Christina felt a hand on her shoulder. She turned and saw Ian. "Why don't you congratulate the colt's trainer for a great race?" As he spoke, Ian looked pointedly at Melanie, who was leaning against the rail with her head lowered.

Christina nodded, moving toward her cousin. "He did a good job," she told Melanie. "He looked a hundred times more controlled than he was last time."

Melanie didn't respond. Christina could see her lower lip quivering. She resisted the urge to glare at Jazz, who was maintaining his distance from the Whitebrook crowd. "You did the best you could," Christina said. She dropped her voice to a whisper. "Now go congratulate your horse and talk to the media. Jazz won't be so quick to sell Jinx if the press shows interest."

Melanie blinked back her tears. "You're right, Chris,"

she said softly. Raising her voice, she added, "Come on, Jazz. Let's go collect our crazy colt and tell everyone how we'll get them next time."

On Friday morning Christina stood alongside Star as Melanie prepared to mount for a short jog. All week Star's breeze times had been solid, although not spectacular. On paper he stood a fighting chance against the other horses entered in the Classic, but Christina knew that races never played out as expected.

Melanie had gone out to dinner with Jazz the night before. When she returned, she had been rather subdued. Melanie had told Christina that Jazz had agreed not to sell Jinx and to give him a two-month break. She had also said that Jazz expected Jinx to be a dominant force on the Triple Crown trail that winter and that any further disappointments would not be tolerated.

"Any instructions, Chris?" Melanie asked. She had insisted on riding Star early that morning even though Christina had offered to work the colt later so that Melanie could see Jazz off at the airport.

Christina shook her head. "You know what to do. Let's just trot him around the track a couple of times. Let him canter if he wants to, but nothing faster than that."

Melanie nodded and moved Star out onto the dirt. Christina watched her colt's fluid movements as he effortlessly circled the track. Star and Melanie were finally in sync. For a brief second she was sure that Star would do well the next day.

That feeling didn't last long. In the next twenty-four hours, the hectic atmosphere of the track became confusion, and it was all Christina could do to keep up. The White-brook contingent met at four in the morning, dividing up tasks so that they could get all three Breeders' Cup entrants prepared.

Ian's son, Kevin, had flown in Friday evening. Kevin McLean was a freshman at Kentucky State. Until recently Kevin had been absolutely focused on soccer, but now he was starting to take a greater interest in training. He had been very helpful during Melanie's early attempts to train Jinx.

Melanie and Kevin volunteered to bathe and groom March to Honor. Christina, who was cleaning tack in front of Star's stall, heard Melanie complaining to Kevin about Jazz as they gathered the grooming equipment.

Star rested his head on Christina's shoulder as she pol-ished the bridle. Christina smiled, gently petting the colt. "I'm glad you don't get nervous before races," she said. "I think I probably worry enough for both of us."

"Good morning, Christina."

Christina looked up to see Brad Townsend walking toward her. "Good morning," she replied politely. "How are your horses doing?"

"Celtic Mist and Light Fandango are ready to go. It seems like your cousin has finally found a way to control Wonder's Star."

Christina nodded. "She's doing a good job with him."

"When do you think you're going to be riding again?" Brad asked.

"My doctor hasn't set a date yet."

Brad reached into his pocket for a business card. "Well, if you ever want a second opinion, here's a doctor you should talk to."

"Thanks." Christina put the card in her pocket. "Good luck today."

"Good luck to you, too." With that, Brad continued striding down the barn aisle.

As she returned to polishing the bridle, Christina kept replaying the short conversation. She didn't think she would ever figure out what Brad was thinking.

Star leaned over and lipped Christina's hair. He also put his mouth over the reins. "Give them back to me, silly," Christina said. She channeled her nervous energy into scrubbing out the spot his saliva had left.

"Hey, Chris, I think you're going to clean a hole right through the leather if you're not careful," Parker teased. He leaned over and kissed her cheek. "How are you holding up?"

"I'm doing okay. I just wish I could be more useful," Christina replied. She momentarily debated whether to tell

Parker about her conversation with his father, then decided against it. Parker usually got upset whenever Brad was mentioned.

"Where's your cousin? I want to congratulate her on Jinx's race."

Christina pointed toward March to Honor's stall. "She and Kevin are busily gossiping in there. I don't recommend going in there unless you want to hear an earful about what a jerk Jazz is being."

Parker smiled. "I think Kevin's better at handling Mel in those moods than I am," he said. "Why don't we go find Allie instead? I'll need her help with Star." Parker helped Christina to her feet.

"Did you get a chance to stop by Willowglen before you left?" Christina asked. She had called the clinic a couple of times to check on Touchstone. So far there had been no improvement.

"Yeah, I went by last night after we talked. The mare looks pretty sick, but Angela kept saying that she'd be dead if it hadn't been for you."

"She might die anyway," Christina said glumly.

"Don't sell yourself short. You gave her a fighting chance." Parker put an arm around her. "Now let's go talk to Allie. I have a feeling she could use some cheering up today."

As they walked to the adjacent barn, Christina felt guilty because she hadn't spent much time with Allie over the past few days. The younger girl must have been experiencing a whole array of conflicting emotions as she watched everyone around her get ready for the Breeders' Cup.

Allie was standing outside Gratis's stall when they arrived. "Hey, guys," she said. "Here to check out the competition?"

Christina smiled, glad Allie felt comfortable enough to tease her. "Actually, I was wondering if you wanted to help with the competition, since you and Parker did such a great job last time."

"Sure. Just let me check with Cindy."

"It's fine, Allie," Cindy called from inside Gratis's stall. Christina moved over to the stall door, petting Gratis when he came up to greet her. Although Gratis had a reputation for being something of a grouch, she had made friends with the colt when she'd been his jockey.

"Are you ready to give Star a run for his money, boy?" Christina asked.

"We sure hope so," Cindy replied. "But I won't be rooting against Star, either."

Christina nodded. "Thanks for letting me put Allie to work."

"Not a problem," Cindy said. "I'll see you in the stands before the fillies' race."

Christina sat on the sidelines as Allie and Parker bathed Star, then helped them with the grooming. They were just finishing up when Mike came up to the stall, telling them that he was taking Charisma to the saddling area.

"You want to come, Chris?" Mike asked.

"I would, but I don't think I'll add much," Christina replied.

"Your mom and I want you there," Mike said. "You really helped Charisma get to where she is today."

Christina nodded. "I'll see you guys up in the stands," she told Parker and Allie.

Parker squeezed her hand. "Tell Mel I said good luck."

In the saddling area, Christina wondered if her parents regretted their decision to invite her. She still wasn't used to watching rather than riding, and since she couldn't do much in the way of saddling, she did the equivalent of pacing with crutches outside the enclosure. However, neither of her parents said anything, so she assumed they understood what she was feeling.

Christina's nerves steadied when she entered the walking ring. It helped that Melanie radiated confidence. "I had a talk with Charisma before the race," Melanie told her. "We're dedicating our victory to you."

Christina balanced herself on her right foot so that she could give her cousin a hug. "Thanks, Mel. Good luck out there."

"You're going to be right along the rail," Ashleigh told Melanie. "Get her out fast, but don't let her burn out too quickly. Keep something in reserve for that last quarter mile."

Melanie nodded tightly as Mike gave her a leg up in the saddle. Christina gave Charisma a pat as the escort rider approached to lead the filly away.

"See you in the winner's circle," Melanie called over her shoulder.

Melanie rode Charisma to a commanding four-length win. Afterward, the media clamored around Ashleigh and Mike, asking about Triple Crown plans. Ashleigh had given her usual polite but noncommittal responses.

Unfortunately, March to Honor was not as lucky. The Breeders' Cup Juvenile was a rough race. Only Light Fandango and one other colt managed to stay clear of all the bumping that occurred down the backstretch and around the far turn. In the end, Melanie and March to Honor crossed the finish line in fourth, a length and a half behind Light Fandango. Melanie immediately launched an inquiry, and the stewards moved her ahead of the third-place horse, who had bumped March to Honor so hard down the backstretch that the colt had nearly lost his footing.

After the Juvenile, Christina left the stands and went to Star's stall. Parker offered to join her, but she declined, wanting some time alone with the colt.

"Remember what I said to you before the Gold Cup?" Christina asked Star as she wiped his face and neck with a sponge. The temperature had risen about ten degrees since the start of the races, and she wanted to keep Star cool for as long as possible. "I was so worried about the Eclipse Award and Horse of the Year honors. Well, I'm not thinking about that anymore. Really, I've realized it doesn't matter. We've been through so much together this year, boy, and I'm proud of us, really proud. No matter what happens today—or even what happens next year—we've done a lot."

"Is the pep talk working?"

Christina turned around and saw Ashleigh and Allie walking toward her. "I think it was more of a pep talk for me than for him," she admitted.

"Well, it's about time for us to get him to the saddling area. But before we go, I wanted to tell you and Allie a story." Ashleigh leaned against Star's stall and absently ran her hand down the colt's neck. Christina noticed that her mother had a faraway look in her eyes, and she couldn't tell whether Ashleigh was closer to laughter or tears. "I keep thinking about my first Breeders' Cup," Ashleigh began. "Allie, your mother had broken her leg a couple of months before, and after auditioning a bunch of jockeys, Clay Townsend chose me as the replacement. The Classic was only my second race. But Wonder made up for my inexperience, and we won. In the winner's circle, Mr. Townsend gave me a half interest in Wonder and all her foals."

Christina closed her eyes, picturing the winner's circle photo that sat in the center of their fireplace mantel at home. It depicted the scene that her mother was describing.

Ashleigh was holding the trophy in one hand and patting Wonder with the other. Despite all the wins she'd had since then, her mother had never displaced that picture.

"There are times when I wonder what would have happened if Wonder's three-year-old season had turned out differently," Ashleigh continued. "So many events had to happen for things to turn out the way they did." Ashleigh straightened, turning to face Christina and Allie. "You're probably wondering why I'm telling you this," she said. "Well, I guess it's because I know you two have also spent a good part of the last few days thinking about what might have been. I wanted to let you know that even though I can't exactly relate to what either of you is going through, you're not alone. Allie, your parents helped me decide to be a jockey. They helped shape me into who I am today. Anytime you want to hear stories about what they were like when they were young, or anytime you just want to talk about them, come find me."

"Thanks," Allie replied. Christina could see that her eyes were bright with tears. Allie made no move to wipe them away. "I wish Mom and Dad were here, but I know that wherever they are now, they have to be glad that I'm with their old friends."

Ashleigh nodded. "We should talk more about this later. But for now, we need to get Star out to the saddling area. You ready, boy?"

Star nickered in reply.

● ● ●

All too soon Christina was back in the stands, watching Star canter in line with the rest of the field. Star's image flashed onto one of the monitors. The colt tossed his head spiritedly, as if he knew he was the center of attention. Christina noted his 20-1 odds. Magic Trick was the 2-1 favorite, and both Storm Rider and Celtic Mist were receiving heavy betting.

Star loaded without a fuss, although Christina could tell that Melanie had her hands full keeping the colt quiet. Christina knew just as well as Mel that Star would need to stay calm until the race began. If he got rattled at the start, he would never get a chance to settle down.

When the starting bell rang, Christina scrambled to her feet, using Parker's shoulder instead of her crutches for support. To her relief, Star broke sharply, and Melanie had him positioned well. They settled into fourth place, about a length and a half behind Magic Trick.

Christina's fingers began moving as if she were holding on to Star's reins. "Hold him back, Mel. Let's take it nice and easy for now," she mumbled. "He's happy and comfortable. Let's keep it that way."

"And the time for the half mile was a fast forty-four and two-fifths seconds. Magic Trick is setting the blistering pace, followed closely by Stronghold and Celtic Mist. Wonder's Star and Gratis are in good position on the outside. Then it's Storm Rider. . . ."

160

Christina half listened to the announcer while continuing to think about each move Melanie must be making on the track. So far it had been a good, clean race.

As the horses galloped toward the end of the backstretch, Christina pushed her hands forward, acting as though she were giving Star rein. "Now, Mel! Let him go!"

Melanie slid her hands down Star's neck, giving the colt his head. For an agonizing second Star didn't respond. Then the colt lowered his head and ran after the leaders.

Rounding the far turn, Star passed Stronghold, moving up into third. Gratis and Storm Rider were hot on his heels.

"Go, Star, go!" Christina added her cheers to the roar of the crowd.

"And down the stretch they come! Magic Trick holds a half-length lead over a fading Celtic Mist, but Wonder's Star, Gratis, and Storm Rider are coming fast!"

Christina felt a surge of pride as Star chased after the leaders. The colt's legs moved so fast that they were just a copper blur beneath him. Christina pushed aside a pang of regret that she was not on Star's back, guiding him in those final, flying strides.

"It's a three-horse race to the finish! Wonder's Star, Magic Trick, and Storm Rider are neck and neck!"

In those final seconds, Christina realized that she no longer cared about the other horses. She focused on Star, who was accelerating with each lengthening stride. It was amazing that this one horse had made her experience such a wide range of emotions over the past three years.

Christina was so caught up in watching Star run that she didn't even realize the race was over. Only the announcer's exclamation that Magic Trick had gotten his nose under the wire a fraction of a second before Star brought her mind away from the track and back to the stands.

A small twinge of disappointment darkened Christina's mood, but she resolutely pushed it aside. Star had put everything he had into that race. He had done everything right.

For a moment Christina just stood there. She saw Melanie waving in their direction as her cousin pulled Star up. Star hardly seemed ready to stop, prancing in place as the escort riders arrived. When Christina finally turned away from Star, she realized that everyone was watching her, waiting for her reaction.

She turned to her mother, giving Ashleigh a big hug. "Thanks for helping me train him, Mom." She then thanked everyone else around her: her father, Ian, Cindy, Allie, Kevin, and Parker. As she hugged Parker and rested her head on his shoulder, Christina glanced up at the television monitor. The camera had panned to her section of the stands, and the commentators were saying something about how disappointing it must be to lose by such a small margin.

Christina laughed at those words. The commentators didn't understand what she and Star had been through. Only the people near Christina did, and they knew why she was celebrating.

It had been a long, hard three-year-old season for Star. But that day the colt had shown his resilience. There was no doubt in Christina's mind that Star would be even stronger when he got back on the track next year. *And I'm going to be there with him,* she thought. *I'm going to recover, and we're going to face the next round of challenges together.*

Christina looked back at the track. Melanie had slowed Star to a walk and was riding toward a gap in the outside rail. Christina gathered her crutches, eager to see her horse. It was time for congratulations. Later she would tell Star about all the plans she had for their future.

Whirlaway is draped with the floral tribute in the winner's circle at Belmont Park, New York, on June 7, 1941, after winning the Belmont Stakes race of the Triple Crown with jockey Eddie Arcaro. Trainer Ben Jones holds the bridle.

Whirlaway

(1938–1953)

Whirlaway, the fifth Triple Crown winner in history, won the 1941 Kentucky Derby by eight lengths, the Preakness by five and a half lengths, and the Belmont by two and a half lengths. In the Kentucky Derby, he set a stakes record that would hold for twenty-one years.

But although Whirlaway showed brilliance at the track, he was a challenge to train and to ride. In his maiden race, the Saratoga Special, the colt bolted to the outside rail while rounding the far turn, yet still managed to win. To prevent Whirlaway from running to the outside, trainer Ben Jones cut away part of the horse's inside blinker. This allowed Whirlaway to see the inside rail but not the crowd or the outside rail. Ben Jones also changed jockeys prior to the Kentucky Derby, choosing Eddie Arcaro, who would later be known as the "Master of the Triple Crown" because he won seventeen of these races during his career. In the closing moments of a race, Eddie Arcaro would avoid taking Whirlaway to the outside so that the horse could not bolt and would instead ride Whirlaway straight through a pack of horses that were slowing down.

Under the guidance of Ben Jones and Eddie Arcaro, Whirlaway finished his racing career with thirty-two wins in sixty starts. He was named Horse of the Year in both 1941 and 1942.

Jennifer Chu grew up reading every horse book she could get her hands on and has been a fan of the Thoroughbred series since she was twelve years old. She recently graduated from Stanford University, where she spent most of her free time riding both English and Western for the Stanford Equestrian Team and competing on the Intercollegiate Horse Show Association circuit. Now a medical student at Washington University in St. Louis, she considers both horseback riding and working with the Thoroughbred series to be great escapes from all the science. This is her third novel for young adults.